PENGUIN MODERN CLASSICS

Fever

SAMARESH BASU (1924–88) was an uncompromising chronicler of the working class. His gritty fiction featured workers, revolutionaries, and radicals who fought society and their own demons and disenchantment. A prolific writer of more than 200 stories and 100 novels, Basu also saw two of his novels briefly banned on charges of obscenity and one win the prestigious Sahitya Akademi award.

ARUNAVA SINHA translates classic, modern and contemporary Bengali fiction and non-fiction into English, and has thirty-four published translations to his credit. Twice the winner of the Crossword translation award, for Sankar's *Chowringhee* (2007) and Anita Agnihotri's *Seventeen* (2011), and the winner of the Muse India Translation Award for Buddhadeva Bose's *When the Time Is Right* (2013), he was also shortlisted for the Independent Foreign Fiction prize in 2009 for his translation of *Chowringhee*. Besides India, his translations have been published in the UK and the US in English, and in several European and Asian countries through further translation.

[illegible]

[illegible]

[illegible] (1894–[illegible]) [illegible] comprehensive chronicle of the [illegible] more than 200 stories and 100 [illegible]

[illegible] contemporary Bengali [illegible]

SAMARESH BASU

Fever

Translated from the Bengali by Arunava Sinha

PENGUIN BOOKS

PENGUIN BOOKS

USA | Canada | UK | Ireland | Australia
New Zealand | India | South Africa | China

Penguin Books is part of the Penguin Random House group of companies
whose addresses can be found at global.penguinrandomhouse.com

Penguin Random House India Pvt. Ltd
7th Floor, Infinity Tower C, DLF Cyber City,
Gurgaon 122 002, Haryana, India

First published in Bengali as *Mahakaler Rather Ghoda* by Ananda Publishers 1977
Published by Random House India 2011
Published in Penguin Books by Penguin Random House India 2016

English translation copyright © Arunava Sinha 2011
Introduction copyright © Shirshendu Chakrabarti 2011

All rights reserved

10 9 8 7 6 5 4 3 2 1

ISBN 9780143425670

Typeset by Le Studio Graphique, Gurgaon
Printed at Thomson Press India Ltd, New Delhi

BRENT LIBRARIES

EAL

91120000350337

Askews & Holts	29-Nov-2017
AF	£9.99

This b... y of trade
or oth... ithout the
publis... an that in
which ... s condition

Contents

A Note on the Title

THE TITLE WHICH Samaresh Basu gave his novel *Mahakaler Rather Ghoda* means 'Horse to the Chariot of Time'. Besides time, 'Mahakal' also refers to the destructive force of the universe—the chariot becomes a vehicle not only of relentless time, but also of annihilation. And the horse that draws this vehicle—anonymous, harnessed to a cause that does not care for the freedom of the beast of burden—represents Ruhiton Kurmi, the protagonist of this novel.

When the novel opens, Ruhiton has for some time been afflicted by a low-grade fever and hoarseness. There is no apparent reason for the symptoms, mystifying the jailed revolutionary. The illness quickly becomes the symbol of the decay, doubt, and despair that assail Ruhiton, haunting him physically and emotionally till the end.

Encapsulating as it does the different kinds of sicknesses—in the socio-political power structure that Ruhiton and his comrades revolted against; in the gradual degeneration of the revolutionary movement; and in the betrayal of the toiling classes by the leaders of the revolution—the fever is the leitmotif of this novel. Hence, it is also the title of this English translation.

Introduction

THE TITLE OF the novel *Mahakaler Rather Ghoda* succinctly captures the brutal irony that is so central to its structure. The title literally means 'Horse to the Chariot of Time', and in combination with the prefatory poem referring to the countless anonymous soldiers without whom the historical transformation underlying the *Mahabharata* would not have been possible, it highlights the tragedy of the subaltern revolutionaries in the Naxalite uprising of North Bengal in the late 1960s. This class, like a beast of burden, pulls the chariot of history and its rebellion is a direct and spontaneous outcome of the daily exploitation that it suffers, and yet it is not given its due in history; nor does it reap any benefits from the revolution. When the Adivasi protagonist of the novel, Ruhiton Kurmi, is released from prison and returns to his village under strict surveillance, he does not meet any of the impoverished peasants; the people who welcome him back as one of their own are either unfamiliar or his former political enemies, trusted supporters of the rich. Even his family members have joined hands with the state machinery.

The Naxalite uprising of the impoverished peasantry was largely led by middle class Maoist intellectuals with remarkable support from the urban student community. These upper class revolutionaries were immersed in theoretical debates informed by the literature of communism while the illiterate, landless peasant understood the same historical situation from his practical experience. The bookish and theoretically engulfed intellectuals differed bitterly among themselves from the very outset—as, sadly, in the history of the international communist movement—exposing thereby fissiparous tendencies which destroyed the movement from within. The subaltern revolutionaries were trapped between the retaliatory violence of the state and the theoretical divisions of the ideologues.

In this sense, the novel brings out the inherently tragic possibilities within the uprising. The uprising gave rise to several first hand/autobiographical accounts like *Communis* by Raghab Bandyopadhyay and popular fiction like *Brishtir Ghran* and *Shaola* by Shirshendu Mukhopadhyay and *Kaalbela* by Samaresh Majumdar. Most of the stories and novels, however, dramatized the disillusionment and psychological debacle of the urban educated youth. In contrast, Samaresh Basu focuses on the perception of the subaltern activist and his tragedy: he was in a way a pawn in the hands of the urban middle class subscribing to a specifically Maoist theory of revolutionary transformation. No doubt many of the elite representatives suffered imprisonment, torture, and liquidation but what happened to the peasants who were the foot soldiers of the revolution? In the 'liberated' areas, the nascent sense of a proletarian identity had been so infectious that the people had turned against traditional habits of drunkenness and wife-battering and the practice of witchcraft. But when Ruhiton returns in freedom to his village and family, he discovers that the community has lapsed back into superstition and obscurantism.

Actually, the movement may have begun in arousal of mass consciousness but not only did it fall apart because of the bickering of the middle class leadership, it also veered towards urban terrorism. As a result, it lost contact with the people to such an extent that it became extremely difficult to distinguish between genuine revolutionary and undercover agent. The underground nature of the movement made police infiltration easy. Thus in the very first chapter of the novel, we find Ruhiton bitterly ruminating about the large number of spies camouflaging themselves among the prisoners like green mountain leeches in the grass or earth-red snakes in the red earth. A greater threat, however, is posed not by disguised outsiders but by cynical and self-seeking insiders.

The author's knowledge of these political realities surfaces at times in the novel; after all, he had played an active role in the undivided communist party before deciding to dissociate himself from it. For instance, he writes about Diba Bagchi—who first taught Ruhiton to dream of a revolutionary transformation—and his strategy of encircling the cities by the villages where 'liberated' areas would be created by a violent uprising. This is no doubt a reference to one of the strategies used in the Maoist revolution in China.

He also goes into some detail about the various categories of landless and semi-landless cultivators. But his focus is really on the changing experiences of the subaltern activist partly modelled on Jangal Santhal, the Adivasi Naxalite leader. He plays down the theoretical debates not in order to deproblematize the novel but to attempt to see the uprising through the eyes of the illiterate subaltern whose knowledge of exploitation is intermeshed with the very business of living. Ruhiton's freedom of spirit is also indicated in his boyhood itself in his somewhat reckless life, often spent in gambling, wild drinking, or hunting wild animals in the forest. His affinity with the untamed primal energies of nature is suggested in the attempt to instill in his pet pigeons the hunting abilities of the hawk, but the project failed because his intoxicated father had killed the birds for food. Does this episode anticipate the futility of the later attempt to create a revolutionary consciousness?

Barring a few exceptions, the educated bourgeois leaders were unable to overcome their class superiority, to give up their vanity of bookish knowledge and to develop a cohesive collective consciousness curbing their habits of possessive and competitive individualism. When Ruhiton is taken to a jail ward where he meets several other prominent Naxalite prisoners, his fellow warriors, the first reaction all around is that of solidarity. Some of the young prisoners openly show their enthusiastic admiration for Ruhiton. But chinks begin to appear as the imprisoned leaders inform him about developments in the outside world. Ruhiton is crestfallen to learn of the death of Diba Bagchi and then of the accusation that he had betrayed the cause of revolution and ultimately served the interest of his landowner father.

In contrast to the middle class leaders, Ruhiton's faith in Diba remains unshaken and he begins to understand the time-serving and slippery tendencies of the educated middle class. The hollowness of the demonstrative solidarity is exposed brutally when the symptoms of leprosy on Ruhiton's body are interpreted by the bhadralok leaders as venereal disease and they immediately want him to be segregated. But that is not enough. Despite their intimate knowledge of Ruhiton's character, they jump to the conclusion that such a disease is not unexpected, given the sexual habits of the lower orders to which he belongs. The divide between elite and subaltern had been perceived even earlier by Ruhiton and his fellow peasants when they were taken to Kolkata to demonstrate mass support for the uprising. Once the show was over, they were simply forgotten and not even given any food despite the presence of many women and children. Mangala, his wife, had, out of her measly savings dating back to her premarital days, given Ruhiton some money to bring back a 'token' from Kolkata, but after this experience Ruhiton refused to do so.

One of the basic stylistic strategies of the novel is the use of laconic and staccato sentences to depict Ruhiton's prison existence. The staccato style builds up an effect of brutality and cramped confinement in a world denying the minimum room required by a human body to remain as a body. It hovers obsessively on the damage done to Ruhiton's body and physical movements by systematic third degree methods of torture. It also captures the disjointed coherence of the stream of reverie interrupted by pragmatic reminders of the present. This style is sharply opposed by the rather hesitant, relaxed sentences describing his life after release. But the opposition is far from the simple one of confinement and freedom. In fact, the stylistic contrast reinforces the irony I have referred to above. Accordingly, imprisonment is less destructive of Ruhiton's spirit than his return into his milieu and family, now drained of all revolutionary consciousness. In the jail, both the policemen and fellow prisoners are in awe of him but once he is freed, Ruhiton finds himself a virtual non-entity at home, ostracized for his leprosy by even his wife and children despite being completely cured of it.

The confinement and the obsessive use of statistics (including the backward and forward movement of the time sequence of those seven days before his release) present the phantasmagoric in chillingly realistic terms, reinforcing, always with an underlying irony, Ruhiton's sense of a rebellious identity and dignity. Life outside the prison becomes by contrast totally unreal and dreamlike, for Ruhiton virtually sleepwalks through this world to his eventual suicide. The taut staccato sentences and Ruhiton's reflections on freedom and proletarian unity in a state of paralysed confinement build up to a climax and then there is a devastating collapse into actual freedom and economic security. Not only is this freedom put constantly under surveillance but Ruhiton had also never wanted freedom exclusive to himself. One might put the matter in a different way: when Ruhiton's limbs are fettered, his mind is free and moving between nostalgic happiness, armed rebellion, and proletarian hope; when his limbs are freed, his mind is fettered by despair caused by the complete sapping of revolutionary ardour in his familiar milieu. Ruhiton's body becomes a kind of text on which we may read the trajectory of the doomed revolution: leprosy thus becomes a submerged metaphor of the diseased body politic.

While Ruhiton's world is drained of colour, the novelist plays on one colour, earth-red, and its suggestion of disease. It is, of course, the colour of blood and a bloody revolution. But it acquires a symbolic plurisignificance. It is the first light of dawn seen through the rear window of the jeep carrying Ruhiton on a mysterious trip that turns out to be an unreal freedom. It is the colour of the flame of the cigarette lighter which takes his mind to the colour of stale meat which in turn is the colour that he repeatedly sees in his fits of fever with blotches on it. His mind is taken back to a feeble snake he had seen long ago which had the same nauseating colour with blotches like sores. This iterative vision serves as a premonition of the tragic fate that manifests itself in the symptoms of leprosy on Ruhiton's body.

In prison, Ruhiton's life is dominated by physical sensations: the excruciating pain of torture, the confinement, the cool breeze of dawn (which he finds rather cold), the smells of damp, solitary cells and of familiar but not quite recognizable flowers, sleeplessness, and so on. In one view, this would suggest a reduction of the protagonist to a mere biological level of existence. But the way these sensations intermesh with his disjointed but never stifled reverie about the past and the future, nostalgia and hope suggests a direct and unmediated mode of knowing the world that is part of his illiterate Adivasi understanding. We may see at work here the relationship in Marxist theory of praxis—knowledge of reality acquired through a direct, transforming engagement with the material conditions of existence—and revolutionary consciousness but unfortunately remains confined to the books as far as the middle class activist is concerned. Ruhiton's physical sensations also raise the revolutionary impulse above mere political calculation to the human instinct for freedom akin to the primal energies of nature.

The relationship with the police officer partially succeeds in breaking down Ruhiton's resolve to a moment of weakness when he expresses anxiety about his family. The officer's offer of a cigarette as a supposedly friendly gesture is repeated several times at different phases suggesting a strange bond between victim and oppressor. Such is the isolation of Ruhiton that the only human relationship left in his life before he meets the prison doctor is that with this police officer. The relationship between body and mind that is crucial to any human identity is also jeopardized. This is isolation reminiscent of the protagonist in tragedy. There are in fact other similarities with tragedy. When the doctor cures him of the disease, he feels that some of his leprosy-affected limbs have fallen off like the rotten branches of a tree but like the tree he will revive: this has the effect of a hope reversed, a peripatetic irony, extending to the futility of the revolution. Above all, Ruhiton partially fulfills the sacrificial role of the tragic hero, if we recall for a moment the anthropological roots of tragedy, wherein the hero takes upon himself the disease that infects society which is healed in his expulsion from community and death. The undermining of the mass movement causes Ruhiton's identity to disintegrate because it was founded on a collective consciousness. Somewhat like the unknown soldiers in the prefatory poem, he performs his crucial role in historical transformation which then ironically relegates him to anonymity and irrelevance.

SHIRSHENDU CHAKRABARTI

Author's Introduction

I DID NOT intend this to be a work of history. Nor of geography. Therefore, my book may have errors in these areas. Are the characters and incidents drawn from reality? No. From imagination? Yes, they are. This story comes from the same place that the writer's imagination does; its outcome is just as fictitious, and entirely personal.

... Behind the Scenes

'Charioteers dispensed advice
Leaders drafted policies
Generals adept at warcraft,
Flawless wielders of weapons,
Proclaimed heroically.
Others, wiser with age and experience
Stayed neutral, distressed
By the terrible war between brothers.

Ah truth! We salute you
Shame on you, you are false!
Each of them appropriated you
For their cause.

They're exalted by history.
How are the armies at Kurukshetra judged?
Faithful to their principles,
To their leaders, they staked their lives
To fight. How are they described? As martyrs?
In the past too they fought, they died
Nameless. Thousands of years later
They keep carrying the flags
Of new ideas, new paths, new viewpoints.
They keep on fighting, the armies at Kurukshetra

Loyal, unquestioning, they battle on
History is created over and over again
Caught between destruction and renewal
What happens to the unsung millions?

Eternity marches on
Relentlessly. Under the yoke
Of time, the horses only
Pull their chariots forever.'

Chapter One

THERE IS A wind which blows in as night breaks into day. It is easy to tell for it has a distinct touch. One can feel it even with one's eyes closed.

Dawn had arrived. It was an old, familiar sensation, for the wind blew through all the seasons. In summer, in monsoon, in winter.

Ruhiton was neither asleep nor drowsy. But his eyes were shut. Whatever sleep he had managed to get was in the first half of the night, on the office bench.

It had been going on like this for three nights. Not exactly like this, but in different ways. Last night he had been shepherded into a car soon after midnight. Yet he had been told earlier that they would leave in the morning. The previous night he had been told that they would depart at dawn.

It had all begun seven days ago. He had come to know from the jail warder on the morning shift that he was being moved to another jail that day. The warder hadn't lied. But Ruhiton had guessed why he had let slip the news. Some time later, that is. The authorities must have tutored—meaning, instructed—the jailer to inform Ruhiton that he would be shifted. The warder from the night shift had been present when Ruhiton was informed, as had been a few prisoners. The prisoners had exchanged glances with Ruhiton.

Barring two, he had not known any of the prisoners prior to meeting them in jail. But the charges against all of them had been of the same kind. Murder, causing injury, robbery, arson, and creating anarchy. And, above all, treason and conspiracy to overthrow the state. Their goals were identical too, therefore they were all fellow travellers. Although Ruhiton wasn't sure whether they were really all fellow travellers, whether they all had the same goals, whether they all belonged to the same party. The very suspicion made him clench his teeth and narrow his eyes like daggers. Hatred flared in his heart. For his experience had been bitter.

The treachery and damage had been horrifying; it could never be avenged. Many so-called fellow travellers had camouflaged themselves like mountain leeches on grass. It was very difficult to tell the spurious apart from the genuine. They lay hidden in the red earth like mud-coloured vipers. They didn't raise their hoods unexpectedly; they didn't coil with a hiss or rise with a lethal spring like the more daring snakes. These mud-coloured snakes and the grass-coloured mountain leeches were imported pimps. They were controlled by the authorities, obeying their signals. They struck furtively.

Ruhiton was cautious, on his guard, yet he wanted to trust everyone, wanted to be friendly with all. But this was impossible with some of the prisoners. He had no choice. But did he himself know why he had exchanged glances with those prisoners or, for that matter, why they had exchanged glances with him, that day, a week ago? His eyes had lit up at the news, as had theirs. Why? And why had Ruhiton's heart started thumping like a drum? Was it out of wild hope? Or a terrible fear?

Fear? He was Ruhiton Kurmi. This was his name. Apparently he had been named by his grandfather, his father's father. Ruhiton.[1] No one knew why his grandfather had named him after a suite of playing cards. His grandfather was a third

---

[1] Refers to the diamond in the four suites of cards.

generation labourer in tea estates. His father was a fourth generation tea garden worker in the Terai. Ruhiton was the fifth generation.

As a child, he had worked on a tea garden for some time. But his father Poshpat—Pashupati—had been the first to quit the tea estate and take up cultivation. Beyond the tea estate, next to the river. Ruhiton had never returned to the tea gardens either. He had become involved in cultivation too, with his father. This line of work meant setting up a home, a household. It wasn't like life on a tea estate. Being a ryot[2] from the Kurmi clan, Poshpat had managed to secure a tract. It was of insignificant dimensions, not big enough to take his name off the ranks of landless cultivators. Tilling the land of the landowners was his real occupation. Still, there was the taste and excitement of reclaiming himself through a change after four generations. There was the hope of settling down, of stability. Not an obsession, but a hankering. A hankering for a household enriched with land, cultivation, settlement. The hankering ran in Ruhiton's blood.

The world knew the name of that place now.[3] Lower, to the southeast of where Ruhiton and his family lived. The wooded area was on the slopes of the waterfall, going up from the sandy beach of the Mechi river in the Terai. Just like the area, the world now knew Ruhiton Kurmi's name too.

Had the warder's deliberate indiscretion—that he would be taken to another jail—scared Ruhiton? There is no fear greater than the fear of death. It is the ultimate fear. But if you kill, you know that you must die too. In battle you stake your life. Ruhiton's fearlessness had not come from the revolution. Ever since he used to lose his way in the forest as a child, playing

[2] A cultivator who owned the land he tilled.

[3] The first violent action of the armed Marxist-Leninist movement in Bengal took place in Naxalbari, which earned it the sobriquet of the Naxal Movement.

hunting games with his bow and arrow, living and dying had become one for him. To kill and to die were synonymous in battle. Just as you had to die for killing someone, you had to live precisely so that you could kill. Ruhiton knew this. Witnessing death had taught him this lesson. Watching his friends die had taught him why he needed to live. Outside jail, death had lurked at every step. Inside jail, it stalked him continuously. Fear meant death. He had banished both from his life.

It was not fear but suspicion that had reared its head. And with it, hope. However faint it may have been, it was still extraordinary. Its name was freedom. Or escape. Or an unexpected opportunity. That was why his eyes had flashed. And the suspicion was of death. They might be trying to get rid of him forever on the pretext of taking him to another jail. This was one of the techniques of elimination followed by the police. On the way from one jail to another, they would set him free in a dense forest, or on the bank of a swiftly flowing river in the dead of night—and then, a few bangs from a gun taken from the belt strapped to a waist. There would be no problems. No one would ever know which jail Ruhiton Kurmi was languishing in. Someone might enquire: 'Which jail is Ruhiton Kurmi in? Which jail?...' In response, there would be an announcement: 'Ruhiton Kurmi has escaped.' This was why his eyes had lit up. In hope and suspicion.

Chapter Two

Ruhiton opened his eyes. After being arrested, he hadn't been able to sleep for a long time. It hadn't been possible either. He had not been allowed to sleep. The interrogation and the physical techniques involved made it impossible. It was possible only when they occasionally gave him sleeping pills. But, recently, he had been sleeping. Like the caged tiger that eventually sinks into sleep, exhausted after pacing up and down. It was the kind of sleep that offers no pleasure, no security. The forests to the north and south and west on the far bank of the Mechi, the reddened earth of the Terai stretching to the horizon, the gurgling of the jungle waterfalls beckoned to him. Every moment of the day. He had on two occasions, in two jails, been beaten till he was unconscious, for giving in to their call. But he hadn't died. His friends had been surprised that they hadn't killed him. Both attempts had been the result of treachery by other inmates of the jail, but amateurish.

Ruhiton was now in a moving jeep. There was no question of sleeping in a moving vehicle. Still, he closed his eyes. There was nothing to look at. Other than the images of four people and four indistinct rifles in the darkness. The touch of the dawn wind at the back of his neck and ears meant night was ending.

He opened his eyes. He could see a hazy red glow. He shut his eyes at once, facing the covered back instead. What was that red glow? He frowned. A stricken expression appeared on his face.

He was sitting with his back against the front seat of the jeep. Arrangements had been made for him to sit on a small wooden platform between the seats at the back of the jeep. Covered with a black blanket, his legs were stretched out before him. His body was also wrapped in a blanket. The blanket had slipped from his shoulders now. He wished they could be covered again. He was feeling cold. He shouldn't have been feeling chilled at this hour. He should actually have been feeling comfortable in this familiar early morning wind. But he was cold.

He felt this way frequently now. Even his body seemed flushed. He couldn't make out whether he had fever or not. He had never told anyone. It had been a year—out of the seven he had spent in jail—since he had been feeling this way. It was not especially uncomfortable or painful. He hadn't felt like telling anyone about it. But now he wished he could cover his shoulders and throat with the blanket. In the moving vehicle the cold bore into him like needles. But he had no choice. Iron chains were clamped on his wrists and legs. The chains around his legs were attached to his handcuffs. He couldn't even bend his knees in this condition. The chains were wrapped around his legs like frames from the groin downwards, weighed down with iron balls. The handcuffs were linked to them.

Ruhiton hadn't been put in ball and chains like these in jail. However, it wasn't as though he had never been chained. After his two failed attempts at escape, he had had to submit to chains for some time. His movements had been restricted. Chaining him now, though, was a temporary measure. He had been put in chains three days earlier as a precautionary measure. Four guards with rifles were in the back with him. All three people sitting in front were armed—the driver and two officers. The chains were to ensure that Ruhiton Kurmi did not attempt to escape while being transferred. Ruhiton knew that even his corpse was preferable to his escaping. At least that would ensure that these people were pardoned. Otherwise they would not be forgiven. Ruhiton also knew that another vehicle was following them. Every police station on the way, too, had been informed.

His uncertainty was not just about the last three nights. To Ruhiton, everything was uncertain. Was he being taken to another jail at all, or would there be more nights such as this one, and then maybe the jeep would suddenly stop somewhere, and he would be made to get off, and then—suddenly…

Ruhiton was prepared for such a situation and such a moment. Because such a situation and such a moment did not spell an opportunity for these people alone. Ruhiton might find an unexpected opportunity too, although he had calculated that they had exactly seven rifles and pistols between them. He had realized something else. The vehicle was not crossing culverts, long bridges, and mountain slopes; almost the entire stretch was flat. Where did such a long, level road lead?

Exactly a week ago, he had been informed of his transfer by the warder. Two days had passed but there had been no news. The jail authorities told him nothing. But their group of friends discussed things amongst themselves. They knew that even if the warder was lying, there was a motive in his passing on the information. They never opened their mouths without a nefarious purpose, never said anything.

Then, on the third day, he had been summoned to the office. He had been informed in everyone's presence that he would be moved to a different jail. Ruhiton had expected to be taken that very night. He wasn't. Instead, after keeping him under armed guard till nine that night, they had placed him in a remote cell in a walled, secluded part of the jail. He had been kept locked up for two nights and an entire day. He had not been allowed to use a toilet outside. A commode (Ruhiton had learnt the name later) on iron legs had been provided within the cell. He was not given an opportunity to bathe. Even his food was brought to his cell.

A few such cells stood next to each other on a plot of wasteland with walls around it. None of the others had been occupied. The cells had been cold, damp. They had smelt of mould and rotting bricks. One warder at a time patrolled the wasteland. Ruhiton had never tried to initiate conversations with them. The warders didn't talk to him either. A single individual used to bring him his food in that deserted cell. He slipped the food in under the bars. He had appeared twice, his face wrapped in a piece of cloth, to replace the detachable iron bucket beneath the commode. He was accompanied by an armed guard. But none of them addressed a word to him.

You cannot fool yourself. Ruhiton hadn't asked anyone any questions, but he was far from indifferent to everything that was happening around him. He didn't know if he really was going to be taken to another jail. Thoughts swirled around in his head. He knew it was pointless to worry. He was mentally prepared to face any kind of event. Event, or rather, accident. But the concerns were inevitable. He tried to guess what they wanted to do with him. There could be several reasons for suddenly isolating him in the same jail. Ruhiton was certain that his friends didn't have an inkling of his being in here. Possibly no one knew—besides the warders, guards, one or two others who came to his cell, and a few of the jail authorities.

'Ruhiton!' A deep voice called out to him from the front of the jeep.

Ruhiton didn't open his eyes. He didn't answer. But his eyebrows and facial muscles contracted, as though he had been dealt a blow. The voice from the front seat was neither harsh nor authoritative. On the contrary, although it addressed him by his name, there seemed to be a measure of respect and amiability in the deep voice, virtually unheard of in such situations. Even without getting a response from Ruhiton, the deep voice asked a question from the front seat. 'Would you like a cigarette?'

Ruhiton didn't respond immediately. But his mouth moistened at the mention of a cigarette. He had smoked just one cigarette since getting into the jeep. He didn't know exactly what time it had been. Might have been midnight, might have been two in the morning. It had been going on this way for three nights. Not exactly the same way. Two days earlier, he had been taken back to the office from his isolated cell after nine in the evening.

Before that, his hands and legs had been chained. Two warders had done the job in the presence of armed guards. That was the only time he had asked in surprise, 'Why are you putting chains on me now?'

'Orders,' one of the warders had answered softly but firmly. Ruhiton had glanced at the guards' and warders' faces in the yellow light in the cell. His clear-skinned, large body had stiffened. All of them had looked grim and unyielding. Their shadows had covered the entire floor and half of the damp white walls. Instead of meeting his eyes, they had thrown cruel glances at him out of the corners of their eyes. But Ruhiton had felt that they were actually neither cruel nor merciless. He believed that they were so intimidated by having to follow orders that they automatically became wooden. They never met the eyes of the Ruhitons of the world.

After chaining him, they had taken him to the office and allowed him to lie down on a bench in the next room. Ruhiton knew asking questions was futile. He had had his dinner already. There was no problem in lying down when in chains. The difficulty was in getting to a sitting position for it was impossible to bend his knees in any way whatsoever. His hands were bound together near his thighs. Ruhiton had fallen half asleep on the bench, as far as it was possible to sleep on a bench. There was the risk of falling off. Drowsy, dozing at times, he had heard this same deep voice calling out to him. The voice that was now offering him a cigarette from the front seat of the jeep.

Jolted awake, Ruhiton had tried to rise from his seat anxiously. 'Be careful! You might fall,' the voice had intervened quickly. Its owner had propped him back up into a sitting position with a hand beneath his shoulder. Ruhiton had glanced at him. He was an officer in a khaki uniform. A holstered revolver was strapped to the belt at his waist. His scalp was practically bare in front, with very little hair. Tall, broad-shouldered, of sturdy build. His snub nose and the wrinkles beneath his eyes gave him a friendly appearance.

But Ruhiton's nose had twitched, his brow had furrowed. He had recognized the officer. There was no reason not to. This was their fourth meeting. The first time he had seen him was ten years ago. The man had been an inspector at the Kharibari Police Station at the time. A junior inspector. He had been thinner then. And had had a full head of hair. But people can usually be identified by their eyes and nose and eyebrows. Three years later, when Ruhiton had been caught after a skirmish, he had met this man again.

Ruhiton hadn't been the only one bleeding. This man had been bleeding too. An arrow fired by someone from Ruhiton's group had pierced his shoulder. It couldn't have been a poison-tipped arrow; else the man would not have survived. Ruhiton's group had been ambushed. They had had no opportunity to defend themselves. Moreover, a large cache of their arms had been seized. This man had brandished his revolver as though he might shoot any of the men in Ruhiton's group instantly. But it was unnecessary. Captured, Ruhiton's comrades were already crushed. They were cowed down by the beating they had received. The attention of the police had been concentrated on Ruhiton. Not that he had declared his name; on the contrary, he had denied his identity. But that had not helped. The man had waved his gun in his face, speaking through clenched teeth, 'If you hadn't been Ruhiton Kurmi, I would have blown your head off by now. I have seen you kill one of our head constables.'

Ruhiton's bleeding face had stayed expressionless. He had looked at the man with blank eyes. He had the same wish, too, to blow his head off. But the actions of the police and their words had made him suspect that they knew a great deal. He had wondered whether someone in the group had betrayed them. How had these people known so much about Ruhiton's party?

Within a few months of this incident, he had met this officer again. Ruhiton had never learnt where the meeting had taken place. It had been a cross between a police camp and an old lock-up. Maybe it was a sub-jail for Kurseong, Kalimpong, or Siliguri. Or the Jalpaiguri Jail. It would have been much colder if it had been the Darjeeling Jail. Ruhiton had been unable to recognize the place. None of his friends had been present either. Only once during his interrogation had he been drawn aside and taken through the trees to a distance. Ordering him to stop at a particular spot, they had instructed him to look to his right.

Ruhiton had seen one of the leaders of his party nearly thirty yards away, smoking a cigarette at a table in a clearing. He was in conversation with someone sitting across the table. Ruhiton had been asked whether he could identify his leader. What leader, Ruhiton had asked. He didn't know the man. He was told that this very leader had revealed everything about Ruhiton. It was futile for him not to confess.

Ruhiton had clenched his teeth and smiled to himself in loathing and rage. He knew they had made it all up, it was all a lie. A trick to plant doubts in his mind. That particular leader had been as solid as a rock, pure. They had arrested him too. He had not run across any of his friends since then.

The interrogation and confessions had continued. He had seen this man once during that time. He hadn't been wearing his uniform then, he was in what they called plain dress. Ruhiton had expected the man to interrogate him, to torture him again. He had been beaten up mercilessly only a short while ago. But the man had said with a smile, 'What's the use of holding back? Why don't you just tell us everything you know? We will get to know everything anyway, tomorrow if not today. We have smashed your fort already.' But he hadn't said, 'We have captured every one of your leaders.' Instead, he had held a cigarette near Ruhiton's head, which had been forced down on a rickety table, asking, 'Cigarette?'

Without raising his head, Ruhiton had looked at him suspiciously. His body was wracked by unbearable pain. Especially in his rectum. A sizeable part of a thick truncheon had been pushed into it and then pressed down like a lever. It was bleeding. He had always been addicted to smoking. Maybe a cigarette would help him forget his pain. But what if the man tried to extract information from him again after giving him a cigarette? Still, he had raised his head and stretched his hand out for the cigarette. The man had offered him a light at once. Ruhiton had put the cigarette between his lips and lit it. 'I'm done here, I'm leaving now,' the man had said, leaving him astonished. He had left immediately.

Then, three days ago, they had met again, late in the night at the jail office. Ruhiton recognized him even though they were meeting after seven years. He had no reason to be happy about the meeting. One look at the man made it clear he was no longer a mere sub-inspector at the Kharibari Police Station. His demeanour, as well as the behaviour of the jail staff, made it obvious that he had been promoted, that he was an officer. Ruhiton could understand these things easily now.

But had the officer not propped him up with a hand against his back, Ruhiton would have fallen to the floor. Besides, why had he smiled that way? Ruhiton felt uncomfortable when a police officer smiled at him in that manner, he felt suspicious.

The officer had not been alone. He had been accompanied by the superintendent of the jail, the jailer, and several others. 'How are you, Ruhiton Kurmi?' the officer said quite casually. 'We're meeting after a long time, aren't we? You and I seem to have something between us, don't we? After all these years, after all my stints here, there, and everywhere, I'm here again as your escort.'

He wasn't lying. But Ruhiton had had no reason to smile like the officer. He had not been amused. Theirs was not a relationship that involved the sharing of jokes. Still, Ruhiton had been forced to acknowledge that this officer spoke and behaved a little differently. He wasn't like the rest of them.

Back in the jail, there was nothing he had had to say in reply. He had risen from the bench. 'There's still five or ten minutes to go, you don't have to get up just yet,' the jailer had said.

'Yes, if you need a piss or a shit get it over with now, Ruhiton. We'll be reaching at first light, there won't be time to stop anywhere on the way.'

He hadn't known the night before last what their destination was, he didn't know it now either. 'I have cigarettes and matches in my trunk, I need them,' he had told one of the warders. 'And I need to go to the toilet.'

Ruhiton's tin trunk was lying under a bare table in the same room. Either the warder or one of the other employees had hoisted the trunk on to the table and opened the lid to hand Ruhiton his cigarettes and matches. Cheap cigarettes. But then, when had Ruhiton ever smoked expensive cigarettes? He had permission to smoke now, however. The jail supplied the cigarettes. Sitting on his bench, Ruhiton had lowered his head and lit his cigarette though he was still in chains. In the meantime the armed guards had received their instructions. Two of them had accompanied him when Ruhiton had followed the warder to the toilet.

Then he had walked towards the gates of the jail, accompanied by all of them. The officer, his companion, the guards, the jail superintendent, even the jailer. As though they were seeing him off at the gate. The rules had been followed without exception. The jailer himself had handed the release documents to the sentry at the gate. Only a narrow door on one side of the gate, wide enough for just a single person, had been opened. Emerging through the gate with the officer in front and the guards behind him, he had seen the jeep. The guards had helped him climb into the back.

Two nights before this present ride in the jeep, too, they had sat in the same arrangement, with Ruhiton in the same position, the officer in the front seat and the armed guards at the back. Before the jeep had left, he had heard some people moving about busily outside, heard snatches of their low-voiced conversation. Someone else had spoken a little louder. The engine of the jeep roared.

Ruhiton hadn't been listening to any of this. With his hands and feet chained, it hadn't been much use listening either. There had been a strange smell. He hadn't been able to make out if it was the fragrance of a flower, or the scent of a leaf, or the odour of the sap from a tree. It was a smell he associated with moving about outdoors at night.

Ruhiton had not expected to experience this smell ever again. In the moving car, he had been unable to identify it. But other images, faces, and familiar smells returned to him now.

Chapter Three

IT HAD BARELY been light the next morning when the jeep had halted at the gates of another jail. Ruhiton had heard another vehicle come to a stop behind them. The car behind them had still had its headlights on.

He had not been informed where they were, or which jail this was. It had looked a little different. It had appeared to be smaller. Here too, he had been kept in seclusion in a remote cell. Ruhiton had realized that the arrangements had been made well in advance. Everything had been prepared. His cell had been well lit, while darkness had hung heavily outside.

'Goodbye, Ruhiton, we'll meet again later,' this same officer had said.

Ruhiton hadn't known where they would meet again. He had assumed this was the jail to which he was being transferred permanently. But he had not made out why he was still in chains.

There were many things about these people he couldn't understand. Although now—at dawn after three nights—it was all looking quite simple.

Ruhiton had been put into the cell early in the morning two days ago. He had spent the entire day there, his meals and the calls of nature had all been attended to inside the cell. His hands had been freed from the chains on his legs. In the evening his hands and legs had again been clamped in chains, after which he had been taken into the office. The office had been crowded with officers and other policemen. All of them had stared at Ruhiton as though he were a mad elephant running amok, now captured and chained. Their eyes had held a hint of fear.

The officer had appeared behind him. 'Are you done with your piss and shit, Ruhiton? We're leaving right away and we won't be able to stop for the next five or six hours.'

'All right,' Ruhiton had responded disinterestedly.

But it hadn't been all right.

'Would you like a cigarette, Ruhiton? Here you are,' the officer had said as soon they had got into the jeep. From the front seat, he had offered the cigarette he was smoking to Ruhiton.

Ruhiton had felt uneasy. All this couldn't be normal behaviour. He had remembered that this same police officer had given him a cigarette seven years ago at a police camp and left. But his suspicions wouldn't be quelled. 'I have my own cigarettes and matches,' he had told him.

'I know you do,' the officer had replied. 'But your trunk will have to be opened to get them. Besides, how will you light your cigarette with your hands chained?'

None of this was untrue. Yet he couldn't let go of his suspicions. It wasn't possible to lift his hand to accept the cigarette. The officer seemed to have realized as much, for he had surprised Ruhiton by wedging the cigarette between his lips. He had lit the cigarette with his own lighter. In the glow Ruhiton had noticed the four armed guards staring at him with stony eyes. His unease had not been dispelled.

'What harm can it do you or me if you were to smoke one of my cigarettes?' the officer had said after lighting his own cigarette. 'Of course, different people's lives never turn out the same way. You have one kind of life, I have another. After all, I could have died at your hands seven years ago.' The officer had laughed as he had spoken. The laughter had not been mocking, as one might have expected. 'But one way or another, everyone has to die one day,' he had continued. 'All of us. What harm can smoking a cigarette do to anyone? Right, Mr Nag?'

The officer was probably addressing the other officer sitting by his side. 'Right you are, sir,' was the response.

Ruhiton hadn't been able to accept this. His ideas about people and the world were different. Everyone would have to die one day, of course. But all deaths weren't the same. Nor were all existences.

'Nobody knows who I am,' the officer had continued. 'But the world knows who Ruhiton Kurmi is. You're world famous now, you know, Ruhiton. It's my privilege that you smoked a cigarette of mine. Right, Mr Nag?'

'Right you are, sir.' It had probably been the officer by his side who had answered.

Ruhiton hadn't glanced backwards—that is to say, at the front of the car. The world knew who he was. Whether this was true or not, it made no difference to him. He had neither been pleased, nor felt any regret. The only reality for him at that moment were the chains around his hands and legs. And the seven armed people surrounding him in the moving vehicle.

He still didn't know—just as he hadn't last night—where he was being taken. Or what his future held. He had no idea whether he was indeed being taken to a jail, or to the slaughtering ground. He was prepared for anything. Still, he kept wondering about the road along which he was being driven that night. Did it run through forests and fields and villages? Or were they travelling through a town? The road seemed quite isolated. Sometimes he could hear the sound of passing cars. Even if they were in a town, it was impossible to tell in the darkness. Maybe some of Ruhiton's friends had noticed this jeep. People from his party were to be found everywhere, after all. But they would never know that Ruhiton Kurmi was being whisked away under their very noses.

Now, at dawn on the third day, Ruhiton had more or less grasped what was going on. Why the morning warder had informed him seven days ago that he was to be taken to another jail the same day. Why no one had told him anything for the next two days, and why he had been taken to the jail office on the evening of the third day and then kept in seclusion in the same jail for the next two days. Since then he had been shifted between different jails at different hours on three successive nights. On the first night the jeep had left with him around midnight or even later. On the second night the jeep had picked him up and left soon after evening had fallen. And last night again the journey had begun around midnight. All of the previous day and part of the night, he had been kept in seclusion in another jail. There was probably only one reason for all this—caution. The plan had been to observe the reaction to the information given to Ruhiton, and then to transfer him safely to the final destination.

North or south, east or west, Ruhiton had no idea in which direction the jeep was moving. But all the activity over the past two days suggested that he would soon be lodged in some jail or the other. They didn't want to move around with him in broad daylight. Everything had to be completed before daybreak. But now, at this moment, he was uneasy about what the officer was saying. The officer was talking of smoking again.

Once upon a time, however, this indeed used to be the time for a routine smoke. Before he had been imprisoned, he used to wake with the birds. He would light up a bidi and go out to the fields. As soon as he returned home after clearing his bowels and splashing water on his face, he would smell wood smoke.

His entire household was under a single roof. The family lived, cooked, ate, and slept in the same room—as did two cows. It would still be dark. But they wouldn't light a lamp. The flames of a fire lit with scraps of wood and twigs in the covered porch would provide the illumination. Mangala would wake up on her own, without his having to rouse her. Using wood and twigs to light a stove of baked clay, she would put the water to boil in an old covered aluminium pan. Ruhiton's mother was a tea drinker. His father, too, when he was alive. Along with his aged mother, her grandchildren would also clamour for tea. But after putting the water to boil, Mangala would disappear to feed the cows.

'Here you are.' He heard the officer speak from the front seat. He felt the touch of what was likely to be a cigarette near his ear. The officer's elbow was probably near Ruhiton's chest as the cigarette came into contact with his lips.

Still, Ruhiton did not open his eyes. But despite his reluctance and unease, he clamped his lips on the cigarette. There was a relationship between smoking and this breeze at dawn that drove away the darkness. All that was missing were the smells of burning wood and cow dung. And many other smells alongside those. Of familiar people, familiar trees, and...

Ruhiton opened his eyes as soon as he heard the click of the lighter. As he lit his cigarette on the flame, Ruhiton took a quick look at the burning eyes of his four armed guards. Did they never close their eyes? They almost never spoke. Their faces were always stern, expressionless. Why did their eyes burn this way? Almost like creatures whose eyes glowed in the dark. And yet they looked sort of harmless, as though they were leashed with chains around their necks.

Ruhiton closed his eyes again. The red flame of the lighter continued to glow before his closed eyes. Not exactly red, but reddish. Like bloodless, stale meat. Not exactly red. Reddish—reddish brown. Was this the real colour of a lighter flame? The burning cigarette between his lips had grown a little damp with his saliva. He enjoyed the warmth of the burning tip. It rose to the edge of his nose, spreading to his face. He was feeling comfortable.

The wind was quite cold. It pricked him like needles on the back of his neck. He would have liked the blanket wrapped around him. The feeling wasn't like the aching limbs and fever from catching a chill after being soaked in the rain. Yet it did feel like a fever. Ruhiton could sense it. But why should he suddenly get a fever? There was no reason for it. It wasn't as though he had lost his appetite. Everything was as it used to be. Yet he felt as though he had a fever every now and then. He didn't feel like a bath at such times and would skip it. 'Got a cold,' he would say if any of the prisoners asked. 'I'll be fine.'

A little chill or a slight temperature was nothing to write home about. But he disliked this reddish haze much more. Ruhiton could see the colour whenever he closed his eyes now. Sometimes he caught a hint of it even with his eyes open. In particular, the colour swam before his eyes whenever he felt a chill and a fever. And he could see red stars or circles against the background of that reddish brown shade. What was it the colour of? Like stale meat with the blood drained out.

He had seen a snake of this colour a long time ago, when he used to hunt in the jungles of Tukariajhar. He had never seen such a snake before, or ever again. The snake had not appeared particularly vicious. It hadn't been very long although it had been quite thick in girth. But even after spotting Ruhiton, it had seemed in no hurry to escape. Nor did it try to bite him. He had gagged when he first saw it. It had had round red spots, like sores, on its body.

Barka, the son of the Nepalese landowner Mohan Chhetri, had been with him. Barka had been carrying a gun. He was an expert marksman. He was also an excellent, though reckless, hunter. He had raised his gun and aimed it at the snake. Still the snake had shown no signs of moving—as though it knew nothing about people or guns or bows and arrows. Its forked tongue flickered now and then. Ruhiton thought the snake's forked tongue had been red too. It slithered slowly along the moist ground, exactly like a caterpillar.

Ruhiton had raised his arm to push Barka's gun away. 'Who needs a gun to kill this thing.' he had said. 'Let it go.'

'What is it? Isn't it a snake?' Barka asked.

'No idea,' Ruhiton had replied. 'I hate the sight of it, the thought of killing it makes me want to vomit.'

Barka had put his gun aside. Picking up a dry branch, he had jabbed at the snake with it. The snake had turned upside down under the assault. It had neither attempted to escape, nor tried to bite. The hideous creature had seemed unable to move. 'This isn't a snake, it's something else,' Barka had laughed. He had struck at it several times with the branch. Still the snake had shown no urgency. Ruhiton and Barka had laughed loudly. Barka had flung the branch at the snake. They had left after that.

Ruhiton had forgotten about this snake (assuming it had been a snake, for he had had his doubts). He had only remembered it now when this horrible symptom had appeared. Whenever he felt a fever coming on, the red glow would appear before his closed eyes. The colour of stale, raw, bloodless meat, and with it, an image of the snake. That same snake, of the same colour, with the red blotches on its skin. He understood now that the snake may have been alive all right, but its skin must have lacked sensation.

Why? Why did this filthy, repulsive creature suddenly appear before his eyes? What connection did it have with his life? None at all. Where had this creature which he had last seen all those years ago, when he was fifteen or sixteen, suddenly sprung from? He was Ruhiton Kurmi—his entire life had more or less turned upside down. Life had flown along a particular course till the time of his father Poshpat Kurmi. The course of Ruhiton Kurmi's life was completely different. He had discarded everything from his old life. He was twenty-two years older now. Had this hideous creature been lurking inside him all this time? How had he never known?

Whenever he thought back on this, he concluded that it might have been better to have killed that freakish snake. It was probably right to get rid of anything that was evil, ugly, and nauseating. There should be no trace of it. He never remembered Barka, did he? Afterwards, he had considered him evil, hideous, and filthy too. He had made no mistake in Barka's case. Was that why Barka's face never swam up before his eyes when he closed them?

Ruhiton opened his eyes again. The back of the jeep was covered. There was a rectangular window of some transparent material like polythene in the thick black fabric cover. If he raised his head and peeped, the scene outside would be visible through it. Ruhiton couldn't see anything. His seat was distant from the window. He sat facing the back, leaning against the front seat. All he could see through the window of polythene was a red glow. Now and then, black shadows flashed past, covering the red glow. Were the flashing black shadows actually roadside trees? And did the red glow signal that dawn was about to break? Perhaps, but Ruhiton couldn't keep bear to watch. With his tongue he flicked away the cigarette, now reduced to a butt. Then he shut his eyes. As soon as he did, the reddish brown colour swam up before his eyes, trembling in his line of sight. A choked sound emerged from him.

'What is it, Ruhiton, did you say something?' He heard the officer speak from the front seat.

'The blanket's slipped off my shoulders, it needs to be put back in place,' Ruhiton said without opening his eyes.

'Are you cold?' He heard the officer's surprised tone.

Ruhiton did not respond. Someone, either the officer or his companion, draped the blanket around his shoulders again. Ruhiton felt a little more comfortable.

'Was your voice always like this, Ruhiton?' He heard the officer speak again. 'I haven't really heard you speak much. I have no memory of your voice. Or have you caught a cold? Your voice is so hoarse, it's almost a croak.'

He was right. Ruhiton's voice did sound hoarse these days. He rasped, as though he had a constant cold. But it wasn't as though his throat hurt. He felt no pain or congestion. Yet his voice sounded hoarse, like a croak, whenever he spoke. Why? Had he caught a cold?

No one knew. When had Ruhiton ever had the time to think of his own health? He had sometimes run up a fever after getting drenched in the rain or roaming about in winter without warm clothes. Both the monsoon and the winter in the Mirik hills in the north were unsparing. It may have been possible to withstand the rains, but not the winter. When he ran up a fever and his body ached, his mother would boil an extract from some obscure bark and vines and leaves and give it to him as medicine. After she developed cataracts, Mangala would do it. Mangala had learnt it all from his mother.

If he fell very ill, he would get pills from the dispensary and have them. But he didn't need a doctor very often. The boiled extract from the bark and vines and leaves used to be good enough. How expensive the pills from the dispensary were! Very expensive! Nor were they available nearby. Besides, Mangala used to practise some kind of black magic… He was reminded of Mangala. Her face floated up before him. When Ruhiton had a headache, Mangala would draw strange patterns on his forehead with a twig. How Ruhiton wanted to laugh whenever she did this. Leaning on his chest, lowering her head, she would mutter incantations, while brushing his forehead with the twig in intricate patterns, starting near one ear and ending near the other. It was as though she were tracing the incantation on Ruhiton's forehead. Did that ease the pain? Possibly not, but he still used to feel a certain comfort in her touch.

Mangala's face floated up before Ruhiton's eyes. Beads of perspiration lined her face. Her eyes were tranquil as always—quiet and affectionate, like a milch cow's. Like mountain lakes, which they called manis, they overflowed with panic whenever she heard her children cry. This was the only way she knew to look at people. She used to look at Ruhiton in the same way. Her eyes probably held a trace of amusement too. When embarrassed, they dropped to the floor immediately. And yet, her eyes always seemed like calm, limpid pools.

'You look different,' Ruhiton heard the officer say again from the front seat.

His voice jolted him back. Had he been thinking of home, of Mangala? Had the officer been talking all this while? Ruhiton had noticed nothing. He didn't respond to the officer; he did not want to talk with him about anything. Theirs was not that sort of a relationship.

But why had he been thinking of Mangala? Why, he even seemed to remember the feel of Mangala on his chest, the scent of her breath. But this should not be happening. Such thoughts were not for him. They only weakened the heart. He had not only staked his own life in this battle. He had staked everything and everyone else too. Mangala was no different from anyone else. No one was. If Mangala thought or acted differently on her own, it had nothing to do with Ruhiton. But Mangala had not displayed any such propensity. In fact, she had been one of them. Most people did not know about her courage. But still, of late—yes, only of late—Ruhiton's state of mind had changed. Now he was often unexpectedly reminded of Mangala, of his children, and of his mother. They would appear before him, complete with their touch and their smells.

Chapter Four

'BUT WHY SHOULD you allow that to happen?' The officer's voice came from the front seat once more. 'If you don't feel well, you must tell the jail doctor. Get yourself treated properly. You have the right. Things are no longer as they were seven years ago, you see. It would have been different if they'd hanged you to death. Of course, you could still be hanged, the charge against you hasn't changed. But if you're ill you have to be treated. I have noticed that your entire appearance has changed. As though you've aged suddenly. The skin on your face—yes, the eyebrows are almost gone too. I remember how brawny you used to look. Like Hidimba or Kichak or someone like that—although you weren't as dark as night...' The officer's tone changed suddenly in mid-sentence. 'Turn your head this way, Ruhiton. To your left. Do you recognize this thing that's passing?'

The officer was talking a great deal this morning, for the first time in the past three days. He was much more comfortable today than he had been in the previous days, as if he was much more confident now. But what was he asking Ruhiton to take a look at? A rumbling and rattling could be heard close to the jeep. It was the sound of something big and heavy. He looked to his left and saw what looked like a small train passing. But there was no steam rising from it. Part of the train was visible. It couldn't keep up with the jeep. Some of the people sitting by the windows of the carriage were looking at the jeep. It was lit up inside as well as in front. Just like in a train, here too, the driver stood up front, wearing a cap.

Large buildings lined the road, their lights still on. The red glow that he had seen through the rectangular polythene window at the back of the jeep actually signalled imminent sunrise. Which meant that the sky was clear today; it must have turned red to the east, its glow spreading.

But what was this vehicle that was running alongside the jeep? This place looked different too, with its large buildings. Ah! In a flash he recalled that this was Calcutta. The vehicle resembled a long tram. A tram! Of course it was a tram! Fourteen or fifteen years ago, or, who knew, maybe a few years this way or that, Ruhiton had been to Calcutta. There was a huge gathering beneath the Ochterlony Monument. A gathering of workers and farmers. This was Calcutta, wasn't it? It had to be Calcutta.

The jeep left the tram further behind. Ruhiton turned his head from left to right. The jeep seemed to have taken a bend in a different direction. It was moving away from the tram. But all these roads, all these large buildings either side of the road, a lamp post at the centre of every crossroad, could only mean he was in Calcutta. This city simply couldn't be Siliguri or Jalpaiguri or Malbazar. Nor Kishenganj or Katihar or Purnea. The tram now lost to his view was the biggest proof that this was Calcutta.

Ruhiton had been to Calcutta just once. It had been a different time back then, the party had been in better shape. He had led a group of tea estate workers and landless farmers. Not that he knew anything about Calcutta at the time. He had looked up to people like Diba (Dibakar) Bagchi, Bhabani Roy, and a few others. They were the leaders who organized the people in the tea gardens and farms in the Terai. Ruhiton had been inducted into the party by Diba Bagchi. He had been entrusted with the responsibility of choosing the people who would join the gathering in Calcutta. Bhadua had also been with him—Bhadua Munda, a formidable fighting force at the tea estates. They had all boarded the train together. They had got off at Bardhaman station the next day. All of them had arrived in a procession at Calcutta. Not just them alone. They had joined many factory and mine workers at Bardhaman. All of them were headed towards the Monument in Calcutta.

It had been a new experience for Ruhiton. There were thousands of women and men. He had been carried away. A sort of heroic happiness had filled his heart. He was certain that something big was happening. It was visible every step of the way. In the raised arms and shouts and joyous laughter of the people lined up on both sides of the road. Arrangements had been made for their meals at different places along the way. Chapattis, vegetables, muri.[4] None of them had worried about food. The excitement had run so high that the thought of eating hadn't even occurred to them. They had reached Calcutta on the afternoon of the fourth day.

Calcutta provided more excitement. Everyone seemed to become more charged as they neared the city. The might of the tea estate owners or of the landowners in the Terai had seemed insignificant. He had felt a strength so immense and powerful that it could have ground any other force in the dust. A certain recklessness possessed him. He was distracted too, by the curiosities around him. This was the marvel of Calcutta. That was when he had seen a tram, with wonder in his eyes. A pole connected the roof of the tram to electric wires. He had heard about it, but he was seeing a tram for the first time. Why should there be steam if it ran on electricity?

The image from his past flashed before his eyes in an instant. He was unprepared for it. This was a tram. So they

[4] Puffy rice flakes, made by heating rice grains at high pressure.

were transporting Ruhiton across Calcutta? There was no more doubt that this was Calcutta. But he was no longer as excited about Calcutta as he had once been.

The gathering beneath the Monument had been massive. People, people, and more people everywhere. But Ruhiton had not been aware of his expectations. He had been filled with a sort of despair as soon as the meeting had ended. Many speeches had been made at the meeting. There had been plenty of applause and loud cries of approval, but after all that it had seemed just like the last day of a fair. On their way back, Calcutta had not appeared remotely interested in them. The night had been spent on the Maidan, on pavements in front of closed shops and at the station. Nobody had stopped them with questions on the way back. No one had shouted out encouragement or offered food either.

Mangala was supposed to have come. She hadn't only because she was pregnant. Ruhiton remembered this now. Diba Bagchi had always been sickly. Along with a few others, he had been permitted to take the train all the way to Calcutta instead of marching with the rest. They had met him in Calcutta. On the way back it was Diba Bagchi who had made them accompany him on the train. One shouldn't say it, but you had to consider whose son he was. He was the son of Dinu Bagchi of Siliguri, famous for his wealth as well as stature. He was an even more powerful landowner than Mohan Chhetri. Dinu Bagchi had a huge farm in Phanshideowa; he was a shareholder in several tea estates.

Ruhiton had himself seen him. He didn't appear to be any more important than a half-naked landless cultivator. For all that he might dress up in a dhoti and kurta, he still plucked at his teeth with a bidi, spat noisily and frequently on the road. His eyes were always bloodshot. He stared at people. He had no relationship with Diba Bagchi, his only son. The rich and famous father had planned to get his son educated and then send him off to supervise the tea estates. Turn him into an Englishman. Pouring cold water over the old man's plans, Diba Bagchi had chosen the opposite path.

Not that Dinu Bagchi could be called an old man. From that point of view the father was more virile than the son. Was this the problem with education, Ruhiton asked himself in surprise. Why else was Diba Bagchi so sickly? As though he were marked by the devil. The father had the strength of ten people. The son was like a frail twig. A thousand illnesses had taken root in his body. But he burst into flames like a meteorite every now and then. Diba Bagchi's strength lay in the fire in his eyes and the things he would say. He had travelled around the tea estates and farms while a student. The police had clapped him in jail within two years of Independence. When he was released after three years, Dinu Bagchi had had his son married with great hope in his heart.

The hope had proved futile. Diba Bagchi had stayed at home for some time. He was a male. The father may have arranged the marriage but the wife was the son's. Just like the soil, a wife was an attraction too. Diba Bagchi had felt this attraction as well. But after presenting about three grandchildren to Dinu Bagchi, he had returned to his old ways. A son of the soil, he had gone back to it. That was when Ruhiton had become acquainted with him. Father and son had not seen eye to eye. He hadn't been able to adjust to the luxury of life in his father's house. Actually, he hadn't wanted to. He had started travelling around the tea estates and farms again. He would never visit his father's farmland in Phanshideowa. Khelu Chowdhury, another leader in the party, did that. Diba Bagchi was older than all of them, however. Those in the know were aware that Diba Bagchi was Dinu Bagchi's son. Workers in the tea estates and farms didn't know this.

Ruhiton had smelt trouble on the way back from Calcutta. How could he respond with the truth if Diba Bagchi were to ask him whether he had enjoyed this huge carnival of theirs in Calcutta? Had Bhadua enjoyed it? Bhadua Munda, the militant leader from the tea estates. Ruhiton hadn't asked any questions. He had observed that no one was looking happy. Everyone's crestfallen expression and eyes had held an anxious desperation to go home. Practically none of them had eaten anything all night.

He remembered that there had been eleven women in the group. Women, meaning wives. They had come with their men. All of them had come from the tea estates. Two of them had had children in their arms. Not all of them had depended on others for money. A few did have some money of their own. Just as well that they did. They had at least managed to feed the women and children at night. But it had to be admitted that even in the dying excitement over the celebrations, many in the group had been curious to see Calcutta. Ruhiton too. And his thoughts had immediately gone back to Mangala.

Chapter Five

MANGALA. IT WAS like the sudden cascade of a monsoon waterfall. All the faces floated up before his eyes—Budhua, Karma, Dudhi. His blind, aged mother. The doctor at Kharibari had said she had developed cataracts in her eyes, which would need surgery. She had no idea what a cataract was, and had never accepted that it could be operated on. Ruhiton did not have enough money either.

His daughter had been named Dudhi, for milk, because her complexion was like her father's. The father had inherited his mother's complexion.

Poshpat Kurmi had married Ganga, daughter of Gajen Santhal from the tea estate. This was unusual—a Kurmi man marrying a Santhal girl.[5] But this was neither Dhalbhum or Manbhumgarh, nor Santhal Pargana. The foothills were occupied by the tea estates of the Terai and the farms. Society and its norms were different here, with caste discrimination being much less. Besides, Pashupati Kurmi had more or less abducted Ganga. Abductions did not take place without cause. When a cow loved a calf she took it into the forest to feed it. His mother had loved his father the same way before they were married.

[5] Kurmis and Santhals are tribes of India. Traditionally, Kurmis live on agriculture, while Santhals live on clearing forests and hunting.

Ruhiton's grandfather had been alive then. Pashupati was still a labourer at a tea estate in eastern Naxalbari. There had been a furore in the tenements over this business of Ruhiton's parents. He used to enjoy all the stories his mother had told him. His father had apparently decided to elope with his mother to Gayabari or some other tea estate in the upper regions of Mirik if they weren't allowed to get married. It hadn't come to that eventually. Ruhiton's grandfather had been an important and venerable figure. He used to mingle freely with other tribes like the Santhals and Oraons and Mahatos, and had very good relations with them. They had come to a compromise. Gajen Santhal had had to pay a slightly higher dowry than usual. Although it sounds unbelievable, he had had to offer two Sikkim cocks. Nobody except the managers at the tea estates and rich landowners or traders could dream of buying Sikkim cocks. Of course, it was different for Marwari traders. They didn't even eat fish.

Pashupati Kurmi had made a big break with the past by abandoning the tea estate. He had been drawn towards land and agriculture. This was a primal desire for a Kurmi. A home of one's own, ploughs and a pair of bullocks, some land to cultivate. Ruhiton's grandfather had harboured the same dream. But he hadn't been able to fulfill it. Even returning to his family home on the border of Bihar and Orissa would not have helped.

But how had an ordinary labourer like Poshpat Kurmi dared to dream of land in an area where every bit of land was already in the possession of officers, landowners, henchmen, and contractors? How much money had he saved? A single officer—a Chowdhury—could have gobbled up Ruhiton's father with ease. The Chowdhurys were Bengali officers who divided and distributed the land, collected taxes, and governed and sat in judgement over everyone. Once upon a time the very name caused palpitations in the Terai region, like a mad elephant would. The Mandals were the right-hand men of the landowners and contractors, worse than even the bloodsucking leeches that clung to the bodies of dogs and sharecroppers.

Ruhiton was filled with wonder at the thought of how much money his father must have saved. Actually Poshpat Kurmi had got into a Chowdhury's good books. No, his father had not even been given the rights of a regular contractor on his land. He had only been given limited rights, the kind accorded to ryots. They lived on the land, they tilled it, but they never acquired rights over it. They had to give it up when asked, had to scram when told to disappear.

But still, how delighted his father had been. The man had even forgotten his hooch for some time. He had shifted overnight from the tea estate in eastern Naxalbari to the south of the Tukariajhar jungle, to the eastern side of the railway lines. Five miles southwest of the tea estates. Below the village of Ramdhan, slightly above Moynaguri village. The mountains and forests of Mirik were visible to the north. The Mechi was within half a mile to the east, marking the border with Nepal. Morang Kaliajhar was on the other side. Bhadrapur was further south.

But the soil? The fragment of land that Poshpat Kurmi got, thanks to the benevolence of Chowdhury Sahib, was within the perimeter of the plot belonging to Mohan Chhetri the landowner. Most of that fragment was white soil with sand mixed in it. There were also traces of black soil. There was no red soil—what was referred to as fallow farmland. In the mountains and the Terai region with its white, sandy soil, black soil was as valuable as diamonds. Even lime was hard to come by. Silt from the river Mechi was brought and spread out on the white soil. And with it, cow dung manure. This was how fallow land was made suitable for cultivation. But it was the black soil which was considered perfect for planting. Corn and autumn paddy grew on it. But it belonged to the landowner. Even the solitary bamboo grove belonged to him.

Poshpat Kurmi had not been cowed down. In a sense he had been nothing but a landless sharecropper. But still he was a ryot. Perhaps he had harboured hopes and dreams of becoming a contractor, even though it had never happened.

From working as a child labourer on a tea estate, Ruhiton had moved to a farm. He used to scoop and carry mounds of silt from the Mechi, where it curved around the cane grove. He would dam the small waterfalls and the narrow canals nearby to store water. He was the son of Poshpat Kurmi, his father's desire ran in his blood too. This desire seemed to have given him a powerful physique. And, looking out at the crops, his mother had felt it was time that Ruhiton married. He had been deeply involved with the Rajvanshis' daughter Tepri at that time. Then Mangala had come…

He was reminded of all their faces, and of their voices, laughing, crying, talking in unison. He could not control the waterfall coursing down his heart. Ruhiton's eyes were still turned to the right. A green slice of Calcutta, curved like a river. A few people here and there. It wasn't clear whether they were strolling or running. In the distance, buildings leaned against the sky. But what he actually saw were the blue forests and the Terai region of Mirik. Ruhiton realized he was saying something. 'I get no news of Chunilal village,' he rasped. 'They don't tell me anything about them. How are they all over there?'

The officer had been about to turn towards Ruhiton. His head seemed to touch the back of Ruhiton's. Just for a moment. Then he asked in feigned surprise, 'Chunilal? Oh, you mean your village, your home?' His head moved away as he spoke.

Ruhiton turned away too, but his body, prickling with the cold, remained alert. A little later, he heard the officer speak from the front seat. 'I have no news of them,' he said with the same casual air.

Ruhiton clenched his teeth. His eyes were screwed shut. Not in anger, but in agony. The anguish of self-hatred was like blindness, unable to see any road to salvation.

The officer was probably right, there did seem to be some kind of a relationship between him and Ruhiton. But that wasn't the only reason for these four meetings. He had not been entrusted with the responsibility of escorting Ruhiton after seven years for this reason. Ruhiton now felt that this man had beaten him every time. This victory over him had been a constant affair. When he had seen this man for the first time ten years ago near the Kharibari Police Station, the man hadn't known who he was. He hadn't given Ruhiton a second glance. The second time, Ruhiton was crushed and defeated, smothered in blood. The third time, when he was being tortured mercilessly at the police camp, and had temporarily collapsed from the unbearable pain, this man had given him a cigarette. But he had not tried to extract anything in return. And, now—at his weakest moment, on this dawn the colour of bloodless stale meat—after three days, the man had kicked Ruhiton Kurmi ruthlessly on the mouth. On the mouth, on the chest.

He was right, the man had made no mistake. Ruhiton realized this now. He had stuck to his position, unlike Ruhiton. He had said many things to him over the past three days. Asked many questions. Laughed. Ruhiton had not reacted. He had not broken his silence then, for he knew that the relationship between the two of them was different. He knew, and, despite the man's incessant chatter, he had kept his mouth shut. But Ruhiton had finally spoken when he shouldn't have. An old memory had suddenly triggered a cascade of rain in his heart. It could not be stopped.

'You've been to Calcutta at least once.' The officer's voice from the front seat was confident. 'You can make out from the tram and the streets that we're inside Calcutta now...'

The officer continued talking. Ruhiton couldn't absorb a thing. A deep-seated anger with himself brought back all the old memories of Calcutta. The day after the meeting, they had marched once more in procession across the city under Khelu Chowdhury's leadership. The procession had ended at a railway station somewhere outside Calcutta. He had met Diba Bagchi there. Diba Bagchi had appeared badly affected by the experience. His face was skeletal—sick, unhappy, angry. Bhadua Munda had exclaimed, 'This is the first and the last time. Never again in Calcutta, damn it.'

Even a man like Diba Bagchi had sat there with his head bowed. He hadn't uttered a word. All of them had been herded into a train in the afternoon. Ruhiton had thought of Mangala as he was boarding. He still had some money in his pocket. He wasn't supposed to have had any. None of them was supposed to have brought any money. But Ruhiton had some.

Before he had left, Mangala had looked him up and down and chuckled. Ruhiton had felt perplexed. Mangala didn't usually chuckle this way. 'What?' he asked.

Mangala wasn't one to explain things. She had been pregnant with Budhua at the time. She was like a fecund cow carrying a calf. 'Nothing,' she had signalled, shaking her head. Nothing? Was he completely ignorant about women simply because he was a farmer? It had been obvious from her chuckle and the way she had looked at him mischievously that she had had something in mind.

'Tell me, no harm knowing,' Ruhiton said.

'Calcutta, after all,' Mangala replied. 'Be careful.'

Was that all that the expressions on her face signified? Ruhiton had knitted his brows.

'What I'm saying is, are you going to Calcutta only for the revolution?' Mangala had laughed.

'Revolution… well, you know. All of us farmers and labourers from all over are gathering in Calcutta to unplug the government's ears. They cannot hear us any more, you see. It's a very big event. Farm and factory workers from everywhere will gather, we'll get to know one another.'

Even this explanation didn't seem to have wiped the curiosity off Mangala's deep, dark eyes. She lowered her eyes in embarrassment, then chuckled again and said, 'It's a big thing, going to Calcutta. This isn't the fair at Bijanbari, after all, is it? Not even Adhikari Baba's winter fair, right? That's why I'm saying you should get something for Ma. A memento from Calcutta.'

Untying a knot at the end of her sari, she had taken out a piece of paper and a few coins and handed them to Ruhiton. Beads of perspiration had appeared on her nose and chin. She had been radiant with a different sort of beauty at the time. Women acquired a different sort of beauty as soon as they became pregnant. It had nothing in common with their alluring looks during the Karam puja—the ceremony that old men and women were forbidden to participate in. Young men and women moved the pine branches aside to perform their own mating rituals. This was a ritual to make women pregnant. But now, Mangala's eyes were sunken, fatigue had taken over her body. It wasn't an illness, however; it was a different kind of loveliness, a pleasing sight, evoking a magical tenderness. Beauty was also a sort of magic.

Ruhiton had looked at the money in surprise. The piece of paper was actually a five-rupee note. It was like a ball of dirty grass, discovered on the road.

Mangala had probably felt a little uncomfortable at the look in Ruhiton's eyes. Slightly taken aback, perhaps. 'I had saved this a long time ago, when I was still living with my parents. I used to work on Master Nasir Mian's farm.'

Ruhiton had not laughed. He had stared in turn at the money in his hand and Mangala's face. But it wasn't as if he didn't understand the slant of what a woman meant—it wasn't as if he didn't understand their smiles and glances. It wasn't like he wasn't aware of the implication of what Mangala was passing off as a gift for his mother or a memento of Calcutta. 'What memento of Calcutta should I get?' he had asked. 'Nose rings or glass bangles?'

'Listen to you,' Mangala had responded intensely, feigning embarrassment.

Ruhiton wasn't one to relent easily. As soon as Mangala had tried to run away he had tugged at her hand. 'What else can I say? I have never been to Calcutta. Tell me what memento of Calcutta to get.'

'I don't know,' Mangala had answered, snuggling up to him.

Ruhiton had thought as much. Mangala could not have responded any other way. There had been no need for an answer either. Lowering his head, he had breathed in Mangala's scent deeply. Her hand on his back and head, she had said in a low, throaty voice, 'May Tista Mother protect you.'

Ruhiton had not bought anything in Calcutta. The next morning, after the meeting, Calcutta had seemed transformed. Bhadua Munda had asked everyone for twenty-five paise in the morning, before the meeting. On the way back, far from offering them food, no one had even asked them if they were hungry. Bhadua Munda and Khelu Chowdhury had collected some food for each of them. And busy Calcutta had looked at them with dispassionate eyes. How different the city had appeared then! The speeding vehicles on all sides and their roar seemed intent on swallowing them up.

Led by Khelu Chowdhury, they had boarded a train around one in the afternoon at a station outside the city. The compartments had been packed with people. Some of them tried to push Ruhiton and his friends off the train. Some hadn't baulked at slapping and kicking them. But they had kept their heads. By then they had been frantic to go back.

To their land of blue forests, where the mountains leaned back against the sky. Where the cool, sweet water from the waterfalls was never miserly like the traitorous trader. Where the grass always grew in abundance, where the farmer's work never ended. But what if it didn't? This was the way of the land here. When landslides took place, families were rocked. Man and beast tried to survive together. After the landslide of rocks ended, there followed a green landslide of harvest on the high banks of the river, The riches might belong to anyone, but there's such a thing as a land of one's own.

At one point during the journey, Diba Bagchi had taken a seat next to Ruhiton on the train. There was no letting up on his cough, nor on his smoking. He had looked like a long-suffering, sick man. Ruhiton had withdrawn into himself. He had not been interested in discussing their expedition to Calcutta. But Diba Bagchi had not brought it up. On the contrary, he had said, 'There's no need to say anything, Ruhiton. I understand everything. You can polish lead and make it shine, but it won't ring out. Am I right?'

This was after Ruhiton's heart. 'You're right,' he had said wih a smile.

Diba Bagchi had been sunk in thought. He had taken frequent drags of his cigarette, coughing every now and then. His cough was terrifying. He had such a small chest. Would the ribcage be able to withstand it? After a long pause he had continued, 'But it won't go on this way forever. All this is just to keep things warm, you see, Ruhiton. I know why it's happening. Not that there's any use knowing.' Taking a drag of his cigarette, he had blown the smoke out through his nose and mouth and coughed, sounding like a flute.

'Stop smoking for a bit now,' Ruhiton had said. 'Give that to me.' He had taken away the lit cigarette from Diba Bagchi.

'Why do you want this one, I'll give you another one.' Diba Bagchi smiled, his face crinkling.

'No need.' Holding the cigarette between two fingers, Ruhiton had balled his fist and taken a deep drag from the opening near his thumb.

'Did you buy anything for your family?' Diba Bagchi asked.

'Buy?' The cigarette smoke had lodged itself in Ruhiton's lungs. 'No, nothing,' he had answered, choking on the smoke.

'I saw some people buying soap and ribbons and bangles and hair oil,' Diba Bagchi had said. 'That's why I was asking. Haven't you brought any money?'

'I wasn't supposed to,' Ruhiton had replied. 'But my wife gave me some as I was leaving.' He had displayed the five-rupee note and the coins in his pocket.

'Are you planning to get something?' Diba Bagchi had asked.

'Oh no,' Ruhiton had said shaking his head. 'I've left Calcutta, I won't buy anything now. My wife had asked for a memento from Calcutta.'

'Calcutta is just a name,' Diba Bagchi had said smiling. 'You get the same things in Siliguri. The prices are different, that's all.'

Maybe that's so, Ruhiton had concluded. Teep for the forehead and alta[6] for the feet were available at the Kharibari shops too. The price of teep and alta at the Jalpesh fair at Gadtali was different, however. Or if you bought something at Adhikari Baba's fair, that wasn't any old purchase either. The price was different. Those were what Mangala called 'mementos'. Every place had a different memento to offer. They reminded you of those places afterwards. But Ruhiton didn't tell Diba Bagchi this.

[6]Teep is a decorative spot or pattern on the forehead, usually used by women. Alta is a solution of red lac used by women to line the edges of the soles of the feet as an adornment.

Chapter Six

MEMORIES OF THE old days returned like the image of his face in the mirror. Once again he was in Calcutta, by the red glow of dawn, surrounded by armed guards in a jeep, with chains on his hands and feet. The more he remembered, the sharper was the pain. Weakness and humiliation cleaved his heart.

Why did he have to ask the officer about Chunilal village all of a sudden? His home was in this village, five miles southeast of Naxalbari. Mangala, his children, and his blind, aged mother lived there. He had not responded to anything that the man had said. Then why did he have to ask this question? Would this officer give him the information that no one at the jail had given him these past seven years?

Had Ruhiton weakened? Had his mind begun to fail along with the fever that had taken hold of him? He had never exposed this weakness. Why today? It had taken several years to mend the broken heart with which he had returned from the congregation of workers in Calcutta. It was Diba Bagchi who had coined their mantra. 'The cities have to be surrounded by villages. The cities have to be controlled by villages. No congregations in Calcutta. After encircling the towns of the south with villages, Calcutta would also have to be engulfed by villages.'

Ever since, Ruhiton had fought to encircle cities with villages. Stake your life, but don't allow the enemy to survive.

Ruhiton had not allowed the enemy to survive. Eliminate and surround, continuously. That was who he was. Why, then, did his heart ache at the thought of his home after seven years? Why, unable to restrain himself, did he have to ask this officer? Was this connected to his fever? Was this why his appearance was changing, why his ears and nose were thickening? Was this why the reddish brown colour of the snake appeared before his eyes whenever he shut them? The one whose skin—the colour of bloodless, raw meat—was mottled with round red spots? Yes, those red spots had started to appear on his body too.

'This early morning breeze should feel pleasant.' The officer's voice could still be heard. 'It should make you feel drunk and drowsy, and here you are saying you're feeling cold. This isn't right. You…'

Yet the man had told him categorically that he didn't have any information of Chunilal village. Ruhiton's head sank to his chest in misery and humiliation. The blanket covering him slipped from his shoulders again. He tried to stretch his legs out further. He slouched lower, leaning against the back of the front seat. But he opened his eyes on receiving a sudden blow from a hard object on his blanket-wrapped legs. He met the eyes of the two armed guards to his right. They were looking at him too. Their gaze was cold, unblinking. The eyes seemed to be red from having stayed open all this while. But why were they blazing!

Ruhiton glanced at his blanket-covered legs. His eyes blazed too. He looked at the two armed guards to his left. They glared at him like the other two. Pressing his back against the seat, he tried to draw his legs in. But he couldn't keep his balance. Both legs twisted to the right from the waist downwards. They fell against the legs of the guards. At once one of the guards tried to straighten them with the tip of his boot.

Ruhiton looked at the guard. He was burning with agony, to which was now added the pain of humiliation. He was Ruhiton Kurmi. His spine seemed to straighten in a flash. Raising himself to a height despite the chains on his hands and feet, he leapt on the guards to his right, butting both of them with his head and shoulders.

The two guards on the left jumped on him at once. Two revolvers were cocked from the front seat, pointing at him. 'What's happened?' the officer asked in English.

By then the guards on the right had pushed Ruhiton back on his seat with blows from the butts of their rifles and their fists. The guards on the left had clamped their hands on him. Blood trickled from Ruhiton's nose and from the corner of his mouth. But he was no longer looking at the guards. He sat with his eyes closed, his teeth clenched.

There had been no impossible idea in his mind. The thick iron frame between his feet, which connected the balls attached to the chains around his ankles, was only six inches long. Each of his feet was over ten inches in length. He couldn't even walk like a clockwork doll. Nor was it possible to stand straight, leave alone escaping, leave alone battling the guards. He had not even considered getting into an argument with them. Why then had he still attacked them this way? He couldn't understand the attitude of the armed guards and some of the warders; what was it that made them mistreat prisoners without provocation? Was it fear of the work they did that caused them to harbour hatred and rage in their hearts? Had it been a different occasion, however, he would probably not have attacked them this way. He was not unaware of how high their degrees of torture could go. A rifle-toting guard like this one kicking Ruhiton's leg away with his boot was hardly a significant incident. Besides, any normal movement was impossible with the handcuffs around his wrists. But still, still, why had he lost his composure?

Ruhiton was answerable to no one but himself. The answer flashed at the corners of his eyes like sparks of lightning. He heard the guards answer the officer in Hindi, 'He was planning to escape, sir.'

Ruhiton knew it was useless to protest. Why protest anyway, and to whom? He did not feel the slightest inclination. He wouldn't make another fatal error like asking for news about Chunilal village. Maybe the guards weren't lying. They may well have come to this absurd conclusion. They couldn't have imagined that anyone in chains could stand up the way he had.

The officer was no longer speaking light-heartedly. His voice was anxious, astonished. 'That's Ruhiton Kurmi for you. It's not for nothing that people call him the terror of the Terai. Right, Mr Nag?'

'Dangerous, sir. Terrific,' Mr Nag responded in English.

Ruhiton could not understand the meaning of the words. Diba babu, Binod Roy, Khelu babu and the rest of them would often use this tone for a particular word—'historical'. Ruhiton had heard it so many times he had memorized it. It must have meant something momentous, just like Behula's song when Lakhindar was bitten by a snake. But Ruhiton had never grasped its meaning. He had never understood whether it signalled fear, rage, or exuberance.

Chapter Seven

THE ENTRANCE INTO the jail for under-trial prisoners was followed by a passage as narrow as a lane. To the left was the gate leading to the women's jail. Their voices floated across the locked gate. Ruhiton observed the large field that came next. A reservoir with steps leading down to the water lay at its head. Two-storeyed wards were situated on the other three sides. There were windows as large as doors on both floors, with thick iron bars on them. A prisoner or two could be seen there, looking at Ruhiton. Curiosity was writ large in their eyes.

Naturally. Old prisoners were always curious when they saw a new prisoner being brought across the field, flanked by two guards. Who was it? What was he here for? Of course, it was a different class of convicts that wondered about this. Pickpockets, thieves, robbers, murderers, thieves, rapists, and other kinds of criminals. He too had been charged with murder, robbery, arson, conspiring to overturn the state, and all kinds of other crimes. But he was different. He did not consider himself a criminal. When people like him saw a new prisoner being brought in, the first question that occurred to them was, which party? Or was the new entrant a floater? A spy, in everyday parlance. Just like a grass-coloured bloodsucking leech lurking in the fields. Or was he one of us?

Ruhiton was no longer in chains. He was walking between two warders, his limbs free. The morning sun was not very hot yet. There was a light breeze, but he couldn't make out where it came from—the south or the east. Dappled by the sunlight, the water trembled under the breeze. To the right of the reservoir stood a large tree with fluttering leaves. They glimmered under the sun. He should have been enjoying the weather. But Ruhiton was still feeling a chill. His skin was prickling as it does during a fever. But he ignored it as always.

The building with a porch near the tree looked as though it might be the jail office. The gate was located that way too. Ruhiton couldn't remember, however, whether he had been brought in that way on a sunny morning two days ago and taken to a building in a different section of the jail. All he was aware of was that the jail was in Calcutta. The incidents that had taken place earlier had left him battered and bruised. But it was not the pain in his nose, face, chest, and stomach from the guards' beating which was unbearable. Overcome by agony and disgrace, he resorted to self-flagellation—why did he have to ask the officer about Chunilal village?

Even that morning two days ago, when he had realized that he had been brought to Calcutta, he had not known the specific destination. Or whether he had been brought to Calcutta for a specific reason. But the chains had been removed that same morning in the jail office. Ah! The luxury of being able to stand up straight without chains on his hands and feet! 'How about a cigarette, Ruhiton?' the same officer had asked him.

No matter how deep his anguish and anger, he had calmly shaken his head in refusal. Without repeating the offer, the officer had said regretfully, 'We were bringing you here quite peacefully. I was happy. Perhaps we shall never meet again. Not perhaps, let's assume we shall not. But why did you have to do something like this when we got into Calcutta. It's all madness where you people are concerned. It's been madness all the time.'

Over the past seven years Ruhiton had mastered one skill particularly well. Being deaf. Not hearing, and not answering, no matter what anyone said or asked. There was no choice. Even the morning before last he had tried not to let the officer's words penetrate too deeply. Instead, he had chided himself even more for having begun to think that this man was different from the others. He had nothing to say in reply. If he had to respond, he would have no choice but to shower him with filthy abuse. He knew perfectly well that the outcome would not have been pleasant. But hadn't it ever occurred to the man to recall how he had responded to Ruhiton's question about Chunilal village? People like him probably didn't want to consider what such a response might have done to Ruhiton. Instead, he had accused Ruhiton of madness.

But yes, what else could Ruhiton's eruption in the jeep be described as? Suffering and anguish were a sort of madness too.

Although Ruhiton wasn't listening, the officer uttered a stream of homilies as he smoked. In the midst of this someone in the office was writing, and asking the officer questions. The man was answering them too.

But Ruhiton hadn't been made to suffer long. Having got his orders, a warder had appeared to free him from his chains and take him inside. He had taken Ruhiton beyond the boundary of the area for under-trial prisoners into the walled compound of another building. There was a space with a canopy over the heads of under-trial prisoners, with iron bars all around it. The space was huge.

Ruhiton did not know at the time that this was where under-trial prisoners were kept in custody. Even at that early hour several of the under-trial prisoners had been brought outside to clear their bowels. There was little scope for privacy in such matters inside a jail. With broad belts in their hands or strapped around their waists, the warder and some mates patrolled the place. There was the stench of urine and faeces everywhere. Some of the prisoners had even called out to Ruhiton, taunting him with questions like 'And who are you so early in the morning, darling?' A few of them had gesticulated with their penises. Ruhiton had glanced at the warders flanking him. They had not looked at those men.

Ruhiton had remained indifferent. He did have a few moments of anxiety over whether he was going to be housed with these prisoners. And the officer's words had kept ringing in his ears, 'Perhaps we won't meet again.' It could be interpreted in different ways. Ruhiton had neither known nor wondered why this had registered with him. Whatever the man's reasons might have been, Ruhiton had hoped that they would never meet again. Even if it meant his being hanged in a cell in Calcutta.

Red roses had bloomed in the walled courtyard to which the two warders had brought him. The yard could almost have been called a garden. Not just roses, there were also other flowering plants. Ruhiton could not identify these flowers. Maybe they were jasmines. Two of the prisoners were working in the garden. They had looked at Ruhiton with surprise and curiosity. A warder was stationed before the door set in the wall. He had opened the door. There were two more warders inside. Ruhiton had felt as though he were entering the bungalow of a junior officer at a tea estate. A couple of structures, which seemed to be a kitchen and a bathroom, were situated on either side of the yard. One had appeared to be a bathroom because next to it, water had been streaming from a pipe leading out of a tank. A two-storeyed house was situated on one side of the courtyard.

Only later had Ruhiton realized that it wasn't a house at all. There were no houses inside jails. The only house was the jailer's quarters. The place he had been taken to was a secluded prison ward. There were ten secure cells on the two floors.

One of the two warders with Ruhiton had carried a bunch of keys. He had been pushed into a cell in the farthest corner of the ground floor and the door locked behind him. The arrangements had been made already. An iron bedstead with a blanket on it, and a commode in a corner. In another corner was a pitcher of water and a glass. There was even a bucket of water and an aluminium pan by the commode. Ruhiton had no idea of the plans made for him. He had quickly stretched out on the iron bedstead.

Afterwards—he did not know how much time had passed—he had been woken by the sound of the iron gate to the cell being opened. A chance to lie down flat, freed of his chains, after three days, had actually made him drift off. Opening his eyes and turning his head, he saw two men in the spacious cell. One of them was in khaki uniform, a cap on his head, a baton in his hand, and in dark glasses. The other was in plain clothes, dressed in a shirt and trousers. He was the one who came closer and said in Hindi, 'Namaste. Where have you been wounded?'

Ruhiton had noticed the doctor's tube, used to examine the chest, hanging round his neck. He spoke with a smile, like a well-bred person. Why had he used Hindi? Polite behaviour was expected, but it instantly raised his hackles. And what wound had he been talking about? 'I haven't been wounded,' Ruhiton had answered in his dialect, sitting up.

The dialect had slipped out. He could speak Bengali just like Diba Bagchi or Khelu Chowdhury. In his own area he was used to speaking in the regional dialect of the Rajvanshis and in Nepali. The dialect of the Kurmi Mahatos of Dhalbhumgarh was also not unknown to him.

The doctor had leaned over to examine his face. 'Yes, I can see dry blood here on the mouth near the nose. Let me put some ointment there,' he had said. Placing a hand on Ruhiton's shoulder, and running the other one over his chest, he had asked, 'You weren't hurt anywhere on this part of the body, were you?'

'No, I haven't been hurt anywhere,' Ruhiton had answered. He had realized that the doctor was there because he had been beaten up by the guards inside the jeep. But he had no aches or pains to speak of. 'If you like, you can arrange for me to have a bath,' he had continued. 'And a hot cup of tea.'

'But you're all flushed,' the doctor had replied with a frown. 'You seem to have a fever. Is a bath a good idea?' He had looked at the man in uniform, as though seeking permission.

'I often have a temperature,' Ruhiton had answered. 'I haven't had a bath for three days. I must have one today.'

The doctor had looked sharply at Ruhiton for a few moments. Then he had turned away to say something in English to the man in the uniform with the cap and dark glasses and baton. The man in the uniform had listened to the doctor, nodding. He had said something, too, in a deep voice. The doctor had turned back to Ruhiton and told him, indicating the man in the uniform, 'This is the jail superintendent. He's here to see y… er… you.' He had started with the familiar 'tumi' for 'you', before quickly correcting it to the formal 'aapni'.

Ruhiton had glanced at the jail superintendent. He wasn't sure whether the superintendent had smiled, or whether it was just his dark glasses that had flashed. He had said something in English to the doctor. The man had a voice as deep as a frog's. He looked formidable too.

The doctor had laughed, saying, 'It really is amazing,' in Bengali. Then he had beckoned to someone outside the cell. A man in prisoner's garb had entered with a box. It was clear from his striped pyjamas and the cap on his head that he probably worked in the jail hospital. Putting the box on Ruhiton's bed, the doctor had opened the lid. Uncapping a vial, he had soaked a pinch of cotton wool in some strong-smelling substance and dabbed it on Ruhiton's face, near his nose.

'I told you I haven't been hurt,' Ruhiton had responded at once, averting his head.

'There's a bloodstain. Let me wipe it off,' the doctor had said.

'It'll be washed off automatically when I have a bath,' Ruhiton had countered.

The doctor had had to give up. He had spoken again in English to the jail superintendent. Then, handing over the box to the prisoner, he had left with the superintendent.

Ruhiton had not had an uncomfortable time in the cell for the next two days. After the doctor and superintendent had left, the warder had taken him outside for a bath. They had given him a hot cup of tea in the passage outside the cell. On both days, his meal had been served in the same passage.

This morning too, he had woken up with the certainty that he would be kept in a secluded cell like this. But now the warders were taking him somewhere else under fresh orders. He had already been informed that he was being transferred to another ward. Ruhiton had not bathed yesterday. Today, despite the chill, he hadn't been able to resist a quick bath. Now he was actually feeling better in this open field with the sunlight and the breeze. People were moving about in the porch of the ward over to the right of the reservoir, in the shade of the tree. They were obviously busy. A couple of warders, along with some prisoners, were scattered across the field.

Flocks of pigeons flew overhead. All jails had pigeons. Ruhiton had come to this conclusion. He had seen pigeons at every jail he had stayed in. Why weren't they afraid of jails? Guards were visible on the roof of the ward, and in the towers higher up. The pigeons were fearless, they were there too. Two pigeons were even perched on the canopy over the alarm bell, primping and bobbing their heads.

Ruhiton remembered wanting pigeons as pets when he was about twelve or thirteen. That was the time his father had left the tea estate in eastern Naxalbari to take up farming in the village. Some of Ruhiton's earnings from the tea estate had already been deposited with his mother. On the occasion of Shivratri, there was a fair at Arish farm, near Ramdhan. His mother had bought him a pair of adult pigeons, male and female, along with four chicks, from the fair.

Ruhiton had built a coop for them with his own hands, using scraps of wood and tin gathered from the village and near the railway station. Many other people in the village, older than him, also had pigeons. They bred pigeons of different kinds—rollers, tumblers, tipplers—which could turn somersaults in the sky and perform other tricks. They raised mixed breeds, but the important ones were the pigeons they bred as hunting birds. Pigeons are not hunting birds by nature, but they could be trained in a way that turned them into cunning, prey-seeking hunters. These would mingle with flocks of pigeons owned by others and lure away the best among them. These pigeons were called hunting birds.

Ruhiton had dreamt of breeding hunting birds like these. Which was why he had learnt to insert his fingers into his mouth and emit piercing whistles. His partner in breeding these hunting pigeons was his younger brother Haratan.[7] Haratan had also been named by his grandfather, after another suite of cards. After him, they had had four sisters in succession.

But Ruhiton's dream had been throttled to death just six months later. Keeping pigeons was like the local saying: The ants will eat it on the ground, the wind will make it fly around. If the pigeons were housed on the floor, jackals would eat them up, if at a height, civets would. So he had chosen the porch,

[7] Hearts in the suite of playing cards.

suspending their coop from the ceiling, beneath the bags of rice. They were visible from the courtyard only if you bent low. The jackals had no way of getting to the pigeons. Nor could the civet climb on the coop to open the barred door. As soon as evening fell, the pigeons had to be put away in their coop and covered.

But one morning, he had found the door to the coop open. Not a single pigeon could be seen. The chicks had been growing well. The female pigeon had laid two eggs. The eggs lay shattered in the straw. Ants were swarming all over the coop, having crawled down from the ceiling. They were there for the broken eggs.

How could such a disaster have happened? Ruhiton had felt tears welling up. A civet? But there had been no sign of one. Haratan had also begun to sob loudly. Ruhiton had strongly suspected a civet;, it couldn't possibly have been a wildcat. A wildcat couldn't have taken away all the pigeons. Besides, it would surely have left signs. But then he had also realized that a civet couldn't have opened the barred door to the coop so skilfully. Was it a thief, then? A thief's handiwork!

Ruhiton's mother had been pregnant at the time. She had been preparing to join his father in the field with her two daughters. Ruhiton and Haratan were also supposed to have been there. His mother had not taken this incident seriously, on the contrary, she had said, 'If they're gone, you can get new ones. I'll buy you six new pigeons from the Tista Mai fair in December. Let's go now, your father's working all by himself. He must be finding it difficult, he'll get angry.'

His mother's behaviour had not seemed normal to Ruhiton. She had neither expressed unhappiness or regret, nor said anything to suggest she was upset about the missing pigeons. She hadn't taken a single look at the coop. Hadn't checked to see what had really happened.

Ruhiton had flung himself to the floor, rolling from the porch down to the courtyard. He had not sobbed like Haratan, he had screamed out curses and abuse. Hearing Ruhiton's filthy expletives and terrible curses, his surprised mother had said fearfully, 'You're actually cursing your own father in this way?'

His own father! His mother had explained. Last night Ruhiton's father was supposed to have sacrificed some pigeons as he had vowed to. Where would he get pigeons at night? So he had taken the ones at home. Vow? Where? There were no rituals or sacrifices in their region at this time of the year. Ruhiton searched every nook and cranny around their house and in the nearby woods. His suspicions had been realized. He had discovered the feathers of the dead pigeons under a pile of leaves. He now knew for certain what had happened. It was the outcome of his parents' drinking deyong, the local hooch. Drunk on deyong, his father had wanted to eat the pigeons. His mother may have tried to stop him. His father wasn't one to give up. He had pulled the pigeons out of the coop, twisted their necks, and plucked their feathers. And his mother had cooked the meat. Who knew how late in the night it must have been.

As soon as he realized this, Ruhiton turned violent. He had run into the field screaming, Haratan by his side. Poshpat had been weeding the fields peacefully alongside others in Mohan Chhetri's farm. This was a big problem in the Terai. As soon as it rained, weeds sprouted everywhere. Cutting them was crucial. But the feast of pigeon meat last night hadn't been a bad one. He was still tingling. The heady feeling from the deyong and the pigeon meat had not left him entirely.

Ruhiton and Haratan raced up in a frenzy, bamboo sticks in hand. Ruhiton had screamed out his father's name. 'Where's Poshpat Kurmi? I'm going to eat the man who ate my pigeons last night!'

Poshpat stood up in surprise, his sickle in his hand. Their mother had followed Ruhiton and Haratan, screaming out warnings to the father of her sons at the top of her voice. Pashupati had taken a while to grasp the situation. As Ruhiton was about to attack him with the stick, he had taken to his heels. Ruhiton and Haratan had given chase. They had picked up pebbles and lumps of earth to throw at him.

All the labourers and farmers working on the field had stood up to watch what was happening, piecing the real story together from the warnings shouted out by Ruhiton's mother. They had started laughing, raising a din. Such entertainment didn't come their way every day. Everyone had egged the two boys on, yes, it was best to kill a pigeon-eating jackal or civet that resembled a human being.

The father could probably have overpowered his sons easily. But he had run away from them out of guilt at having stolen their pigeons and eaten them.

Chapter Eight

'WHERE ARE YOU going? Come here!' said a voice in Hindi. Ruhiton felt a prod on his back.

He came to a halt. A small plain door lay ahead. There were walls on either side; a narrow, dank, shaded passage lay in between. The ceiling was low enough to scrape your head against if you stood upright. With one warder in front and another behind, Ruhiton entered the narrow passage. His heart was filled with misery. Memories of the old days hurt him. He didn't want to recall the past. He didn't want to remember the life that lay behind him. He didn't want to think about it. But the memories kept flooding back. The old life and the people in it. And when they did, a dam seemed to burst within him. The misery was unbearable.

The warder in front stopped. The door set in the wall on the right was closed. It didn't have iron bars. It was made of thick wood. An iron rod stuck out of the door at an angle. As soon as the warder gave it a shake, a sound rang out on the other side. A section of the door, a few inches wide, opened at once. A pair of eyes peeped out. Ruhiton and the warders returned the gaze. The opening, smaller than a birdcage, closed; the eyes disappeared. There was a rattling of a bunch of keys or chains inside. The door opened.

The doorstep was a raised block of cement. Ruhiton stepped over it as he followed the warder in front of him into the room. The warder behind him also entered. The door closed again. A different world lay in front of him. It was still a jail. And yet…

Thirty or forty yards away from the door was a space like a room, with a roof and walls. To the left was a long canopy. Ruhiton didn't count the number of trees standing on both sides of the courtyard, which was long and wide. The entire place was covered, cool. Prisoners were scattered here and there. A clear stream of water gurgled down the middle through a canal with paved edges. Huddled near the door on the right, a few prisoners in uniform were deep in discussion. Some—Ruhiton didn't check how many—warders were milling about. Almost all of them had turned towards Ruhiton's group at the sound of the door opening and closing. Most of their eyes were questioning, radiating suspicion.

'Ruhiton Kurmi! Ruhittton!' An elated cry rang out, breaking the air of silent suspicion hanging over the courtyard.

In the blink of an eye a figure raced up to Ruhiton. Wrapping his arms around Ruhiton with all the force he could muster, he shouted again at the top of his voice, 'Ruhittton! Comrade!'

Ruhiton had already caught a glimpse of his face. Khelu Chowdhury! He had heard earlier that Khelu Chowdhury had been caught. Just as he had heard that Diba Bagchi had also been caught. He hadn't believed it. Now there was no choice but to believe it.

The excitement and exhilaration in Ruhiton's heart was no less. He had not met such a close friend and party leader in a long time. These were the people who had shown him the way. Everything had started with them. Many more had joined in afterwards but the relationship with these people was special.

Ruhiton also wrapped his arms around Khelu Chowdhury, hugging him to his chest. He didn't shout, his voice sounded like a groan. 'Oy ohey Khelu babu! Ah! Khelu babu hay!'

Chapter Nine

VIRTUALLY ALL THE prisoners scattered inside the ward and in the courtyard surged forward to gather around Ruhiton and Khelu Chowdhury. The warders were looking somewhat nonplussed. One or two of them were smiling, however. But they were outnumbered by cold eyes and stern faces. Their expressions reflected wariness.

Most of the prisoners' eyes had widened in amazement. There was deference and respect too. Ruhiton heard someone nearby whisper, '*The* Ruhiton Kurmi? From Naxalbari? I had never dreamt of seeing him in person. My life is now worth living. Long live Comrade Ruhiton Kurmi!'

'Long live Ruhiton Kurmi!' several voices echoed loudly.

'Stop shouting. No one is allowed to make a noise here,' a deep voice was heard issuing the command.

'Shut up. We'll burn the place down if you stop us,' responded a few aggressive voices in protest.

'Don't forget who's here,' some more voices roared in support. 'This is Ruhiton Kurmi. Mahatma Gandhi stayed in this ward. Now Ruhiton Kurmi is here too.'

As soon as he heard this, Ruhiton raised his face from Khelu Chowdhury's shoulder and looked at the others in surprise. His smiling eyes held a question. Mahatma Gandhi—this was the one name with which his life had no relationship. They were as different as day and night. He had heard of Gandhi baba as a child. He had seen his photograph. Among the many pictures on the walls of the labourers' shanties at the tea estate was one of a smiling old man in glasses. There was probably a red or white tilak on his forehead. He was bare-bodied. There was something of a resemblance between the picture and Chowbey the grocer. But the smile? The smile was even lovelier than his grandfather's. People didn't bow before this photograph without reason, Ruhiton had concluded. Chowbey wouldn't be able to smile this way even in a dozen lifetimes.

Ruhiton had heard of Gandhi baba from his father and grandfather. They showed their respect when they mentioned his name by raising their hands to their foreheads. But Ruhiton had been more interested in Lebong in the Darjeeling hills. Not to watch the horse races in spring. He had heard from his father that revolutionaries had tried to assassinate Bengal's Governor 'Annarson'—Governor General Sir John Anderson—there. Ruhiton was eight years old at the time. The country was ruled by the British. The police had gone on a rampage for some time across the hills of the Terai and the Dooars.

The incident was engraved in Ruhiton's memory. Why? This was a unique trait of his character, he didn't know the reason himself. It is always preferable to eliminate the enemy. He had never articulated this to himself, but the principle operated in his blood.

Ruhiton had gone to Lebong. Not by car or train. When he was fourteen or fifteen, he had dressed for the trip and, along with his friends, climbed up the mountainside along a steep trail. They had climbed all the way to Lebong as though it were a game. Lebong, via the tea estates of Mirik and Jor-Bungalow.

A few years later had come the strike by the railway workers in Darjeeling. Not a single railway engine had run in the entire Terai region. Not a single wheel of a train had turned. Ruhiton's blood had tingled as he slathered silt from the Mechi on the field. Why? The company sahibs, Marwari and Bihari traders, Bengali Rajvanshis, and Nepali landowners had all become enraged. Having defeated their eternal enemy for once, the poor had felt their blood pounding in their chests. Ruhiton had not been aware that he could have responded to these events this way. Diba babu and his group had staged protests in the hills and in towns at the time. Another group had been involved in the railway strike. The success of that strike was engraved in his memory. So were many subsequent events.

But the acts for which Ruhiton now stood accused of—murder, robbery, arson, and conspiracy to overturn the state, along with several other charges—explained his opposition to Gandhi baba. Ruhiton knew that they were adversaries because of their divergent viewpoints and methods. Still, the news that Gandhi baba had stayed in this ward evoked wonder in him. Ruhiton had heard that he had waged a different kind of battle against the British, termed the path of non-violence. Ruhiton knew of no equivalent to it. He too had been on fast several times during his seven years in jail. And apparently Gandhi baba was the one who had passed on this weapon. Although Diba Bagchi would say sometimes, with a mixture of anger and mockery, 'How can fasting be a form of agitation? This is nothing but a quarrel between the prostitute and the client. The prostitute goes on fast when treated badly by the client. Then the client coaxes the prostitute to break her fast. If you forget the medicine for your skin you can get ill in other ways. All this is a prostitute-and-client type of agitation.'

Initially Ruhiton had agreed. Diba Bagchi and Khelu Chowdhury were experienced at fasting. But Ruhiton was not as convinced today. In jail he had realized that fasting could indeed be a weapon. And he had got results. People like

Ruhiton had no choice but to resort to fasting to secure their rights in jail. Everyone in his party had accepted this by now.

Not only had Ruhiton never seen Gandhi baba—his foe in ideology and in method, a man with whom he had no relationship—with his own eyes, but he also knew nothing, understood nothing, about Gandhi baba except his fasting. But still, he was a great man, all told. His photograph wasn't the only proof of that; people respected him like a god too, and all of this had convinced Ruhiton that he was an important person. 'Mahatma Gandhi stayed here too?' he asked with a surprised smile.

'Yes, apparently he used to pray beneath that tree every day.' One of the prisoners pointed the spot out to him.

'So what?' said Khelu Chowdhury. 'You, Ruhiton Kurmi, are even greater for us.'

'Long live Ruhiton Kurmi,' someone said.

'Long live Ruhiton Kurmi,' other voices echoed at once.

'Why are you behaving this way here, Khelu babu?' one of the Bengali warders said. 'There'll be trouble any moment. Why don't you talk inside the ward? You know very well slogans are not allowed here.'

'We'll raise slogans for Ruhiton Kurmi even if you beat us to death,' someone roared.

Ruhiton wanted to calm everyone. He was enjoying this fervour but he didn't want a riot to be sparked off. He knew what it was like to be beaten up without having the means to defend oneself. He didn't want to create such a situation.

Supporting Ruhiton, Khelu Chowdhury said, 'All right, never mind the slogans now. Ruhiton bhai has only just arrived, let's receive him first. We have our greatest pride Ruhiton bhai amidst us today. Let's get all the news first.'

Pushing and shoving ensued. 'Introduce us to Comrade Ruhiton Kurmi, Khelu da,' the prisoners said in unison, falling in line with Khelu Chowdhury's proposal.

'Of course I will,' Khelu Chowdhury said. 'Come, let's go inside.' Turning to Ruhiton, he asked, 'Ruhiton, don't you have your things with you?'

'I did have a trunk,' Ruhiton said, looking around as though he was seeking someone out.

One of the warders came forward. He was holding the tin trunk.

'Then they will let me stay with all of you, Khelu babu?' Ruhiton asked.

Khelu Chowdhury laughed. So did most of the prisoners. 'Why else would they have brought you here?' Khelu Chowdhury said. 'They've brought you here under orders. Else we would never have got to know you'd been brought to this jail. When did they bring you here? From where? So many rumours have been floated about you here…'

'Khelu da,' someone called out before he could finish. Although it wasn't threatening, the tone was apprehensive, watchful. Khelu da was being warned not to open his mouth in the presence of the warders.

'I was brought here day before yesterday in the afternoon,' Ruhiton said meanwhile, slipping into the dialect of his region.

'Here?' Khelu Chowdhury exclaimed. 'Day before yesterday? Where did they keep you?' He glanced at the warder. The one who was carrying Ruhiton's trunk.

The warder didn't reply. His small eyes signalled annoyance. He had a baton under his arm; it was obvious from his lower lip that he had a wad of tobacco in his mouth. 'Where will he stay then?' he asked in Hindi, referring to Ruhiton.

'Why don't you tell us what your orders are?' Khelu Chowdhury replied, his face hardening.

'I've been ordered to deposit him in this ward.' The warder continued using his own language.

'And still you want to know where he'll stay!' Khelu Chowdhury spoke sarcastically. 'You want to create trouble, I can see.'

The warder transferred his baton to his hand. Another warder said in Hindi, 'There'll be no trouble, Khelu babu. Take your friend inside, or find some other place to sit. Your friend will stay here in No. 12, there's nothing to ask or discuss.'

'We certainly have nothing to discuss,' said a young man standing next to the warder. His lips were curved in anger, his eyes blazed. 'It's this warder who's talking nonsense,' he continued.

Glancing at the young man's face, the warder stiffened; putting the trunk down, he retreated a step. The prisoners suddenly seemed full of rage. The warders exchanged glances with one another.

'This warder is probably a landowner back home,' someone quipped.

Some of the prisoners laughed at this. Khelu Chowdhury and Ruhiton too. 'Never mind, let it go,' said Khelu Chowdhury. 'We'll demand that this warder should not be sent to this ward any more. Come away, Santu.'

Santu was the young man standing beside the warder. The situation had clearly become charged. The general workers and prisoners had also stopped whatever they were doing to stand up. Santu and several other young prisoners had turned rigid, steely-eyed. Santu had already been chained and put in solitary confinement twice after getting into scuffles with the warders. The warders always remained vigilant with him. But as soon as Santu moved away under Khelu Chowdhury's instructions, the situation eased.

Taking Ruhiton's hand, Khelu Chowdhury began to walk off towards the ward, saying, 'Come inside, everyone, we'll get to know one another there. But...' He paused, then continued,

'Ruhiton, you seem to have quite a high temperature. And you look different.'

'I have no idea what it is,' Ruhiton said lightly. 'Every now and then I feel as though I have a fever. My skin feels hot, you know. And it's breaking out in sores and boils. The doctor at the last jail used to put some sort of ointment on it. It didn't help at all. Who knows what medicines they make me take? I feel quite sick, you know, Khelu babu. By the way, you know that place in this jail for—what do you call them—under-teral or something?'

'That's right, the under-trial jail custody,' said Khelu Chowdhury.

'Yes, probably,' Ruhiton said. 'They took me through that place day before yesterday afternoon to a small jail building. A two-storeyed prison.'

'Gora digri,' one of the warders said.

'Yes, I've heard this jail has a ward for Europeans. They call it the gora digri. I've never seen it. Oh, so they brought you here day before yesterday? And finally you're here in this ward today. Here we are, Ruhiton bhai, through this door here. The stairs are to the left. Let's go and sit upstairs.' His voice changed at the end.

The prisoners jostled each other as they tried to enter the ward along with Ruhiton and Khelu Chowdhury. A crowd ended up blocking the narrow door. It was difficult for even two people to enter together. Everyone was excited at seeing Ruhiton Kurmi. His was a special name for all of them.

Two or three of the youngest prisoners, no older than seventeen or eighteen, squeezed past Ruhiton and Khelu Chowdhury and turned back to stare at Ruhiton with wide, curious, shining, exhilarated eyes. They walked backwards towards the stairs, even climbing them backwards, staring all the while.

This long room downstairs was shaded, darkened even in broad daylight. Several barred windows, as large as doors, looked out on the field. Some light filtered in through these windows. But this light was feeble, barely illuminating the room.

Ruhiton glanced at the young prisoners. He knew the look in their eyes. He had seen eyes glowing with excitement in the same way among young men of this age in other jails. He had spoken to them. Most of these people wanted to hear of the battle. They wanted to hear how the police had unexpectedly surrounded their den, how this had been followed by a battle between guns on one side and bows and arrows on the other. Budhua, his eldest son, must now be as old as these boys. Karma was almost the same age. He must be grown-up like them too. Would they stare at Ruhiton in the same way if they saw him? At their father?

'Did you hurt yourself, Ruhiton bhai?' Khelu Chowdhury put his arms around Ruhiton on the first flight of stairs.

Some people lower down on the stairs also extended their arms towards him to prevent him from falling. Ruhiton had not noticed the first step. He had not been looking at the floor, actually. Had he even been looking at anything inside the ward? His eyes had not been trained on anything in the real world. The faces of two boys named Budhua and Karma, which he had last seen seven years ago, had swum up before his eyes. They had now appeared before him as young men.

'No, I'm not hurt,' he replied. 'I didn't notice the step. The room is dark.'

But there was an agony of regret in his heart. Why had he remembered his sons? This happened to him so often these days. He was reminded of his home, his wife, his children all the time, in different ways. He was Ruhiton Kurmi. Why should he have these weaknesses? Could someone who had staked everything in his life for the revolution possibly have a past? Or memories? Why could he not accept such an inevitability?

'Here, let me help you,' Khelu Chowdhury said. 'But it's not all that dark here.' He looked at the other prisoners behind Ruhiton with a frown, his eyes surprised.

Khelu Chowdhury's surprise was reflected in the eyes of the other prisoners too. But that was momentary. It was possible to miss one's step in an unfamiliar place.

The steps were far more clearly visible to Ruhiton now. They rose in a straight line, without curves. He was unable to hear Khelu Chowdhury's last statement. Nor could he quite make out what the people behind him were saying. He could only hear things said in his immediate vicinity. It was best if he could watch their faces and lips while listening.

There was only one reason for all this. Ruhiton knew it very well. Little things had shown him that his ears were no longer as sharp as before. Once upon a time he could hear a dry leaf falling in the depths of the forest. He could hear a footstep far away the way a snake does, from faint vibrations in the earth. He could identify an unknown voice wafting in on the wind from the distance. He used to be as alert as a bird at night.

After his capture, the random beating he had received at the hands of the police during interrogation had probably damaged one of his eardrums. Just as he thrust his lower abdomen out a little while walking because a bone near his anus had cracked. There was pressure on the cracked bone if he tried to stand straight when he walked. It hurt. There was pain even if he walked with his abdomen thrust out. But much less. But he could still hear many sounds that were as faint as that of a dry leaf dropping in a forest. At other times, he could turn stone deaf. Especially when it came to those whom he didn't want to listen to.

The ward upstairs was much brighter. The field and the reservoir were visible through the barred windows, as large as doors. The sunbeams hadn't yet slanted enough to enter through the windows. They would as soon as the sun rose a little higher in the sky on the east. There would be more light everywhere in the room. The trees and the jail office on the other side of the tank could all be seen through the windows. There were large barred windows on the opposite wall too. The courtyard of the ward lay in that direction—the courtyard which Ruhiton had crossed with the others to come up into the ward. The presence of a few trees dimmed the light slightly. Still, there was much more light on the first floor.

Two rows of iron bedsteads were laid out for prisoners along the length of the ward. There was nothing between the rows. Blankets were laid out on the bedsteads. Khelu Chowdhury made Ruhiton sit down on his own bed.

A young prisoner had carried his tin trunk upstairs. 'Where should I put Comrade Ruhiton Kurmi's trunk, Khelu da?' he asked.

'Where will Comrade sleep?' asked another before the reply could come.

'Right here in our ward,' Khelu Chowdhury said. 'Since they've sent Ruhiton bhai here, they'll send a bed for him too. His bed will be placed wherever all of you want. Put the trunk somewhere for now.'

Ruhiton's eyes met the prisoners', which shone with curiosity and expectation.

'Each of us will want comrade Ruhiton Kurmi's bed to be next to his,' one of them said.

Everyone laughed. Ruhiton Kurmi's heart overflowed with happiness and pride. 'We'll stay together, all of us,' he exclaimed. 'This room is for all of us.'

'That's right,' many of them spoke up exuberantly. Meanwhile everyone had sat down on two of the iron bedsteads, crowded against one another, contorting their bodies, leaning towards Ruhiton.

'Oh, how long it has been, Ruhiton bhai.'

'Yes, tell me the story of your arrest first,' Ruhiton said. 'As far I knew you were at Padam's set-up, north of Shanilal the landowner's house. We had met about an hour earlier, right? And after that? I've heard many different stories about you over the years. Some said you had escaped. Some said you'd been captured. Others said you'd been shot dead. And still others said you'd been hanged. There was no way of knowing what was true. I hadn't imagined for a moment I'd see you here. Now tell me the details, will you?'

'Why, didn't Padam say anything?' Khelu Chowdhury asked with a smile.

'Oh no, that's where the problem is,' Ruhiton said. 'When they brought Padam in half dead, I thought that since they had been to his set-up in the forest, possibly no one was alive. I had heard gunshots from that direction. From Padam I heard Santosh had been shot dead before his eyes. And that you had fought bitterly with a loaded gun. Padam didn't see which way you went.'

Khelu Chowdhury's expression tightened. His forehead creased. The smile on his face was of anger and scorn. 'How would he have seen me,' he answered. 'If I could have, I'd have told all of you to run. I had seen from Padam's set-up that they had surrounded us. They had blocked all the roads with jeeps and trucks. They outnumbered us by a mile, each of their guns had bayonets on them, and obviously they had flashlights for hunting at night in the forests. The headlights from trucks and jeeps had turned the whole place as bright as day. In that light I saw them swarming all over the place. I saw Ruknuddin Chowdhury the landowner among them, he was talking to the bigwigs. I don't know who else was there. There was no doubt that the details of our hideouts were on their fingertips. We would not have been able to fight our way out of there. Besides, many of us were missing. Several people had gone to headquarters that day, remember?'

Ruhiton's eyes were fixed on Khelu Chowdhury. But his gaze seemed to go beyond Khelu Chowdhury. Nor was his mind in the jail. His heart had travelled to a night seven years ago in the forest below the Mirik Police Station. Still, he nodded at once in response to Khelu Chowdhury's question, saying, 'Hmm, hmm.'

'I think they had information too,' Khelu Chowdhury said. 'That's why they surrounded us overnight and ambushed us suddenly. I saw that there was no option but to fight my way out of there. I told Padam this. He paid no attention, he couldn't be controlled. I escaped in the direction of the Tukariajhar jungle. After spending the night there, I crossed the Mechi and set off for Morang in Nepal early the next morning. That's where they captured me.'

Ruhiton's enormous eyelids had no lashes to speak of. His bloodshot eyes grew redder in surprise. 'You were captured in Morang?' he asked. 'Inside Nepal?'

'Yes, inside Nepal.' Khelu Chowdhury smiled. His smile was like a curve in a red-hot iron rod. 'I had thought I couldn't be captured easily if I went into Nepal. I had planned to return after a few days. But I was captured when I reached Morang. I was having a cup of tea at a roadside shack in the evening. Suddenly someone called me from the back, Khelu da, you here! I didn't have the chance to turn. I didn't even see the people who pounced on me. There was a blow to my head. I couldn't even pull out the gun at my waist before I fainted. Knocked out. Then...' Khelu Chowdhury didn't finish what he was saying.

Ruhiton still appeared distracted. The others listened with blazing eyes, as though they were trapped in an incredible dream. Nobody said a word. Only one of them said through clenched teeth, 'Betrayal!'

'No doubt about that,' Khelu Chowdhury said, his smile much more relaxed now. 'Tell us about yourself, Ruhiton bhai,' he continued. 'But let me introduce everyone to you before that.' He proceeded to point to each of the prisoners and announce their names.

Ruhiton looked at everyone in turn. It was impossible to look at his eyes for any length of time. Because they had no lashes, his eyelids looked like livid sores. Even his eyebrows had lost most of their hair. They were barely there and the skin was cracked. There was hardly any hair on his head. The thick bush of hair from seven years ago was gone. But like before, even the sparse hair that emerged from his scalp was of shoulder length. The skin on his face seemed thicker than usual. His nostrils were dilated, with a bulbous red swelling on the tip of his nose. The bridge of the nose had subsided, as though it were broken. His earlobes were unnaturally thick too, as were the edges of his ears. There were still two thick little sticks running through his pierced ears, however. His chin and forehead sported round red blisters.

Ruhiton Kurmi's appearance made it difficult to identify him at first. But then it didn't take long to know who he was from the rest of his features. His complexion wasn't very dark. It tended towards the fair. This had not been completely ruined yet.

After the introductions, the prisoners said in unison, 'We want to hear Comrade Ruhiton Kurmi's story now.'

'Yes, start with where they brought you here from,' said Khelu Chowdhury. 'Seven years' stories to be told.'

'I'll tell you everything,' said Ruhiton. 'But tell me a few things before that. Are all of you exempt from labour here?'

Khelu Chowdhury and the rest looked at one another sombrely, as if none of them had the answer. Eventually Khelu Chowdhury himself replied, 'You can never say for sure, Ruhiton bhai. From fasting to other things, a lot of effort has gone into this. One group of our people has been kept separately from us, somewhere in this same jail. We don't get any news of them. They haven't given us any physical labour for the past few months. But you never know when orders may be changed.'

'Which means it's the same system everywhere.' Ruhiton shrugged. 'And what about the foxes in the holes? Do they visit you?'

'Not any more,' a young man named Sukumar answered instead of Khelu Chowdhury. 'Three or four of them used to, and the moment they ran into us, we'd have fights. Later on, however, we used to be more at the receiving end of the beatings.'

'You can rest assured, Ruhiton bhai,' Khelu Chowdhury said laughing, 'the foxes are in their holes. They won't visit the jail any more. They're publishing newspapers to explain the party line on the revolution, and sharing votes between themselves. They will leave their holes to move into pigsties.'

Everyone laughed. 'I see,' said Ruhiton, 'there's nothing wrong with the party line.' Everyone laughed again at the way he spoke. He continued without laughing, 'And Diba babu? What news of him? I heard at a jail in Bihar that he had been captured.'

Everyone looked surprised, their eyes questioning. They glanced at Ruhiton Kurmi, and then exchanged glances with one another. 'It happened just the other day,' Khelu Chowdhury said with astonishment in his voice. 'Diba Bagchi was captured, then he died. His heart failed, apparently. He didn't have to serve time in prison like the rest of us.' He sounded unmoved.

'Diba babu's gone?' Ruhiton said, stricken. His enormous lashless, reddened eyes looked like festering sores. Everyone's faces vanished, while Diba Bagchi's face blazed before his eyes. His oldest revolutionary friend, the one who had shown him the dream of a new life. The dream whose fulfillment had seemed certain—a world in which even the blind would have regained their sight, the mute would have spoken, barren women would have given birth, the landless would have land of their own, labourers would have run the country! For the first time in his adult life, Ruhiton Kurmi experienced grief. He shut his eyes. Diba Bagchi's face remained before him.

Chapter Ten

THREE NIGHTS LATER, one morning, Ruhiton suddenly stopped in his tracks near one of the walls of Ward No. 12. The sun was up. Many of the inhabitants of the ward were downstairs. Through the windows, the sunlight could be seen glistening on the green blades of grass in the field, on the water in the reservoir, on the leaves of the banyan tree in the distance. Like the world, the jail too had awakened. According to its own rules, in its own way.

The double-barred gates to the ward downstairs were locked at eight in the evening. Prisoners ate their dinner before that, under the canopy in the courtyard. The gates were locked after they were shepherded inside. The lights were put out in the ward. There were temporary toilet arrangements within the ward for the prisoners at night. The railing on the staircase went up all the way to touch the ceiling. There was also an iron gate at the bottom of the stairs. This too was locked after the prisoners had been packed off upstairs. Nobody remained in the ward downstairs, only the lights were kept burning. The eagle eye of the night patrol swept this empty ward too. The jail stayed awake all night, from one end to the other, to the stomping of boots, the sound of whistles, the slow shouting of the night patrol.

At dawn the gates were unlocked. That was when the prisoners used the toilets and bathrooms outside.

Many of the prisoners had gone downstairs after the gates had been unlocked in the morning. Ruhiton Kurmi stood near a wall of the ward. Two of the convicts were preparing to take his iron bedstead downstairs. Two other convicts had brought this bedstead upstairs for him in the same way four days ago. Surprised, he asked why it was being taken away. 'Orders,' came the reply.

Some of the other prisoners, including Khelu Chowdhury, stood on one side. Ruhiton looked on with his lashless, virulent red eyes. The convicts were now clearing away the other bedsteads so they could take away his. Ruhiton could not protest. His friends weren't protesting either. This was the first such incident during the seven years he had spent in jail. His surprise was changing to anger. His anger was being replaced by despondence and trepidation. He watched, Khelu Chowdhury and the others watched, the convicts dragging the bedstead towards the staircase. Ruhiton asked them anxiously, as though he had suddenly remembered, 'Where are you taking that?'

'Downstairs,' replied one of the convicts.

Ruhiton glanced at Khelu Chowdhury and the others again. What should he do? Should he protest? Should he attack the convicts—'extras' in jail parlance? All by himself? Was it possible to protest alone? When one's companions remained inactive, uninvolved, unwilling? This was a new experience in Ruhiton Kurmi's life. Everyone's attitude towards him had suddenly changed. The warm welcome, the excitement and enthusiasm had disappeared. Ruhiton couldn't recollect exactly when the smiles had been wiped off his friends' faces. But their friendly expressions had changed at some point.

Was it on his first morning in this ward? When Ruhiton had clasped his hands on his chest, saying, 'Oy ohey Diba babu' in a soft, distressed, voice. He had not wept, his eyes had shed no tears. But his heart had cried out in grief. He had never grieved so much for anyone else in his life. He had been unable to speak for a long time.

But before he could say anything more, Khelu Chowdhury had said dispassionately, 'What's the use of mourning for Diba Bagchi?'

'Mourning happens on its own, Khelu babu. No one forces you to mourn,' Ruhiton had responded.

'But what's the use of this mourning, Ruhiton bhai? You knew very well that Diba Bagchi was Dinu Bagchi's son.'

Ruhiton had looked at him in confusion. Khelu Chowdhury's eyes were glittering with rage. Several other pairs of eyes were looking at him the same way. Ruhiton had wondered whether the world familiar to him all his life had been turned upside down. Why was he being told all over again that Diba babu was Dinu Bagchi's son? Khelu babu had snarled when he had mentioned Diba babu's name! Hadn't they been bosom friends? Hadn't Diba babu been their leader?

'Comrade Ruhiton Kurmi.' Someone else, not Khelu Chowdhury, had spoken up. 'Dibakar Bagchi was a hated landowner's son. His children and wife are very rich, they're living in great comfort. Dibakar Bagchi was a leader of the poorest of the poor. Now tell me, what kind of luxury are your children living in? Which landowners' riches are they living off?'

This had had no effect on Ruhiton. Nor had his astonishment been dispelled. 'But friends,' he had said, 'the whole world knows Diba babu was the son of a very big landowner. But he had distributed every last bit of his father's land among ryots and sharecroppers. Hadn't he?'

'Whose land was it, who distributed it?' a young man had asked sarcastically. 'The land belonged to Dinu Bagchi. Did Diba babu hand over the ownership documents to the sharecroppers? Did his father grant him that right? It's easy to distribute the entire world among the poorest of the poor verbally.'

'How can there be documents for such distribution, Comrade?' Ruhiton had asked in surprise. 'Diba babu said so, and the sharecroppers occupied his father's land after fighting for it!'

'And as soon as they were forced to leave after losing the battle, the land was back with its original owner. The sharecroppers were beaten to death, and Dinu Bagchi is living a comfortable life. '

'Is that Diba babu's fault?' Ruhiton had said. 'Why put him on trial after his death?'

'The question of a trial had not risen then, so there was no trial,' Khelu Chowdhury had replied. 'That's how our party works, you won't be absolved of guilt simply because you're dead.'

Ruhiton hadn't been able to contain his surprise. 'But you accepted Diba babu as your leader, Khelu babu,' he had said.

'I did,' Khelu Chowdhury had snapped. 'I don't any more. He himself was a class enemy, which was why he led the party in the wrong direction.'

Ruhiton had already known that there were cracks in their old world. He was aware of the loathing and anger they felt for one another. He felt a deep anguish. Who was a class enemy? Just who? Khelu babu's father had fat shares in many tea estates. He didn't know what these young comrades owned. Leading the party in the wrong direction? Did no one realize it earlier? Or was Diba babu's corpse under fire today because his leadership had not been successful? Ruhiton could never consider Diba Bagchi a class enemy as long as he lived. 'But Khelu babu, Diba babu was our leader. I will grieve for him forever, I cannot deny this,' he had said in a hoarse, distressed voice.

Khelu Chowdhury had been silent for a moment. He looked at everyone. With a smile he said, 'I won't blame you, Ruhiton bhai, it's not your fault. You'll understand things gradually. With time you'll understand everything.'

Ruhiton had barely been listening to Khelu Chowdhury. Diba Bagchi's face was still vivid in his mind's eye. The news of his arrest and death had driven every other thought from his mind. Was that when everyone's faces began to change when they looked at him?

'But where will I go?' Ruhiton almost screamed. 'I have not been told.'

Khelu Chowdhury spoke at last, looking at him. 'You'll stay in the downstairs ward from now on. The doctor has said you should be separated from everyone else.'

'Separated?' Beneath the unhappiness, there was a distraught note in Ruhiton's response.

'Yes, separated,' Khelu Chowdhury answered.

'Why?' Ruhiton asked in the same voice.

Khelu Chowdhury's lips curved like a dagger. 'Haven't you looked at yourself?' he said. 'What are those sores on your hands and feet and face? Can't you make out from your nose and your ears? But I don't blame you for this.'

Blame? Ruhiton asked himself in surprise. He knew of the dried sores on his hands and feet and face. He knew of his flaming eyelids, his flared nostrils, the collapsed bridge of his nose, the gradual thickening of the skin on his face. Even the tips of his fingers and toes were inflamed and withering. He was using the oily ointment given by the doctor at the previous jail. He knew he was ill. He had a fever every now and then. His voice had become hoarse. He couldn't hear clearly. His nose often ran without his realizing it. His fingers would neither straighten, nor bend. Only the edges remained curved and stiff. They looked like the hairless paws of a bear. But blame for what? And why did he have to leave his friends? The doctor here had neither been to see him, nor told him anything.

'I haven't done anything wrong, Khelu babu,' Ruhiton said in surprise. 'Why should you blame me?'

'You weren't always the Ruhiton Kurmi you are now. That's why I don't blame you,' Khelu Chowdhury said. 'Only you can tell whether you've inherited the illness or acquired it yourself. You had a lot of fun with Mohan Chhetri's son Barka Chhetri once upon a time. You wandered around fairs, listening to all kinds of music, gambling. Didn't you?'

'I did,' Ruhiton admitted in a flat, surprised voice.

'Try to recall the other kinds of pleasure there. You drank hooch and spent Barka Chhetri's money to buy the company of young whores. Now those whores are bursting out through your blood.'

'Oy Khelu babu, what do you think you're accusing me of?' Ruhiton didn't shout, didn't snarl. He emitted an agonized scream, sounding as if an axe had plunged into his chest. 'Are these their marks?' He spread his hands out before his eyes. All of this seemed to be the demon's tricks from his earlier life. All these things Khelu babu was saying! This sickness in his body. Tepri's face suddenly floated up before his eyes. Tepri, the daughter of Shuku Pongani, a small landowner in Chunilal village. His girlfriend at sixteen.

Why had Tepri become his girlfriend? He didn't remember. When he was sixteen, Ruhiton used to till Shuku Pongani's land. How old had Tepri been at the time? The same age as Ruhiton, or a little younger. Tepri was married by then. There was no reason not to have been, given her age. Ruhiton could not fathom why Tepri used to roll her eyes, why she used to curve her lips in a smile, why she used to undulate her hips as she walked by, so close that he could actually feel a breeze. Even if he could fathom, he didn't dare. The landowner's daughter! But he liked her. His blood would tingle. Tepri's swinging breasts would make her sari drop off them. The bow in Ruhiton's heart would be drawn taut. Everything about Tepri excited him. The way she walked, the way she talked, the way she flirted, the way she smiled sweetly. But she had ringworm on her skin. She couldn't have avoided it. Everyone in Shuku Pongani's family had ringworm. Even their cows had sores, probably from ringworm.

Ruhiton looked at his arm. The red bulbous marks were everywhere, starting with the elbows. His palm was like a hairless bear's paw, the tips of his fingers were withered. Had he got these marks from Tepri's ringworm? He had slept with her in the jungle. Such intense pleasure. He hadn't remembered the ringworm. From Tepri's skin, the ringworm had also passed to his skin. How many families were there without ringworm sores? Ringworm ointment sold no less than snacks at all the fairs. Ruhiton had bought ringworm ointment from the Behubari fair. But Tepri was not a female crab he had paid to sleep with. He had been accused of getting these sores from whores at the fairs he used to frequent with Barka Chhetri.

'But I don't blame you, Ruhiton,' Khelu Chowdhury repeated. Your forefathers were porters on tea estates. You were a landless...'

'Quiet! Be quiet now,' Ruhiton roared. Distorted with rage, his voice rang loudly in the upstairs ward. His raw eyelids were flaming red. His entire body flushed red.

Khelu Chowdhury and the other prisoners were dumb-struck. They looked both fearful and curious at this sudden outburst. Ruhiton came forward, one step at a time. But his flaming, bloodshot eyes were now trained on the staircase. Khelu Chowdhury and the other prisoners reared back, expecting an attack.

Ruhiton stopped in the middle of the room. He threw a glance at Khelu Chowdhury. And then looked at the staircase again. Meanwhile, the convicts had taken his iron bedstead downstairs. Ruhiton walked to the head of the stairs. Holding on to the wall with his right hand, he lowered his head and began to descend, one step at a time. A song he had heard his mother sing when he was a child came back to him. He chanted the lines in his head:

Clouds gather in the north
It's raining in the west
All the fine clothes are soaked.

Was this how life was? Clouds gathered in the north but it rained in the west? And one's beloved clothes, full of colour, became drenched? A fire raged in his heart. Its flames burnt him more than any anger could. A dam seemed to burst in his heart. Mucus trickled out of his nose. He wiped it with the back of his hand.

At the bottom of the stairs, he stopped abruptly.

His bedstead had been laid out in the ward downstairs, next to a window looking out on the field. One of the warders was looking at it. The two convicts stood close by. All of them turned to look at Ruhiton. Ruhiton could still see his mother's face. He could still hear her sing, 'Clouds gather in the north, it's raining in the west...'

Chapter Eleven

'Bring the trunk downstairs and put it next to the bed,' the warder ordered the convicts.

The convicts looked at the staircase. Ruhiton was still standing at the bottom of the stairs. The convicts looked at him apprehensively. Ruhiton decided not to raise his head. The sight of several shadows on the floor told him that Khelu babu and the rest were leaning over the banister to watch him.

Whores. On Barka Chhetri's money? Fun at the fair! He was reminded again of all the things they had said. After Tepri there was Mangala. His father had himself paid a dowry to Mangala's father for her marriage with Ruhiton. Ruhiton had told Mangala about Tepri after they were married. But not by choice. He had confessed his adventures after an overdose of deyong. After the hangover had passed, he had become aware of Mangala's rage. Which other girl had he known besides Mangala? Yes, he had never forgotten Tepri. But he had never seen Tepri after his marriage to Mangala.

Tepri belonged to the Rajvanshi tribe. They could not marry Mahatos, Kurmis, or Santhals. But she could have married Ruhiton if she had been a Mahato or a Santhal. It would have been called a baha samha wedding. That was what they called it when a widow or a married woman married another man. Ruhiton had heard this from his mother.

He did not know the rules of marriage among Rajvanshi Kshatriyas. Tepri had never spoken to him of marriage. She only wanted to run off into the jungle, shaking her hips. Besides, her father was a small landowner. Ruhiton was his hired tiller. But what if Tepri had been a Mahato or Kurmi or Santhal, what if she hadn't been married?

Lying beside Tepri in the dense shadow under a wistful breeze, deep inside the forest, if he happened to ask why she didn't want to go to her husband's home, she would hum a song:

'Shon baahe dewanir chhaowa
Mui kambakti kapal pora
Shoshur hoia mayeo khaowailen mokey
Shashur hoia dilen kannya
Mairley golam dupurbela
Mairley golam maatit phyaleya.'

(Listen to me O minister's son, I am an unfortunate fool. My father-in-law had me beaten up. My father-in-law instructed the servant. He threw me down on the ground in the afternoon and beat me up.)

Tepri seemed to be sobbing along with the wind in the forest.

Without looking around, Ruhiton went outside the ward. The prisoners who were already downstairs looked at him. Ruhiton didn't look at any of them. He walked off towards the shade beneath the tree. He had forgotten where he was.

He could have had a nir bolok bapla with Tepri, he mused. He had learnt of all this from his mother. A nir bolok bapla was the kind of wedding where the bride forced herself on the groom and his family. Tepri was the kind who would force a man to marry her. This force was the sweet honey of her existence. But Poshpat Kurmi had been alive then. Having observed Tepri for a couple of days on Shuku Pongani's farm, he had realized what his son was up to. Before the year was out he had arranged Ruhiton's marriage. Kirin baha bapla. A straightforward wedding. He had chosen the bride himself, borrowing the money for the dowry. And he had made Ruhiton give up his job on Shuku Pongani's farm.

Still, had Ruhiton really managed to forget Tepri? He had not thought of her at all for some time. That's what human hearts are like. Mangala had made him forget everything. Tepri and Mangala were different. Mangala was younger too. A simple, straightforward Mahato girl. She was not yet a woman. She didn't roll her eyes the way Tepri did. She had not learnt to smile bewitchingly. She ran away if Ruhiton tugged at her hand. There were no ringworm sores on her skin. Her dark complexion was so fine it seemed soaked in oil. Her eyes were as deep as the black waters of the Chandmani Mai lake.

Yes, when the torrents from a waterfall filled up the bottomless pit of a lake, it was called a mani. Mani was also a synonym for a woman's senses. The lake was a symbol of the mother's womb. And people worshipped this symbol. They prayed for plentiful water. Actually, the Terai was a natural reservoir for potable water. Water was available round the year.

Ruhiton used to feel as though his seventeen years of existence had been submerged in Mangala's eyes, which were like the deep, black water of the lake. But could it stay submerged forever? Why then had he gone off in search of Tepri after all those years of being married? Was it like a tiger stalking the kill it had left behind? Like the tiger who couldn't help revisiting his kill?

No, Ruhiton had not run into Tepri again. Mangala had been the only one in his life after that. Just the one wife. But so many different personalities in the same form. Many in one. Why talk of Tepri alone? He had discovered every woman in the world within Mangala. What an experience it had been.

But whores? He had been accused of bringing this disease on himself by sleeping with whores at fairs, financed by Barka Chhetri? As these thoughts ran through his mind, he raised his hands to look at them. The very next moment he flashed a look over his shoulder at the ward on the first floor with his flaming red eyes, the wounds festering on the eyelids. He gritted his teeth so hard that his jaw trembled. He didn't see Khelu Chowdhury by the window.

The agony was greater than the anger in Ruhiton's heart. How could an old-timer, a leader of men, hurt him so much? Was their long relationship a lie? Whores? Paid for by Barka Chhetri? Oh! You were right, Ma. Clouds gather in the north, it's raining in the west…

He leant against a tree, putting his weight on it. There was no one near him now. The roar of a passing heavy motor vehicle could be heard close by. He shut his eyes. And still the colour of stale raw meat floated before his eyes. Against this background wriggled the familiar reddish-brown snake with the red welts on its skin.

Ruhiton started, opening his eyes. He felt as though the snake was wriggling around inside his body. Was that why he saw it every time he shut his eyes? An image of Barka with his gun appeared before his eyes.

'Here you are.' A Bengali warder stood before him, his baton dangling from a thong around his wrist. The look in his eyes made Ruhiton's skin prickle. Although he had a smile on his face. 'This is where Gandhiji used to pray,' he said, 'when he was in this jail.'

This was the spot! But unlike that man, Ruhiton didn't know any prayers. How did praying help? Did the oppressed become free? Did the landless get land? Did workers run the country? Was this agony, this burning rage and humiliation, abated?

Turning away from the warder, Ruhiton set off towards the shaded part of the field near the western wall. 'Come with me,' said the warder. 'I came here to fetch you. The doctor is here to see you, he's waiting in the downstairs ward.'

Ruhiton stopped abruptly. Turning back, he set off towards the ward after a glance at the warder. So Khelu Chowdhury had got them to send for a doctor?

Chapter Twelve

As soon as he set foot inside the ward, Ruhiton saw a young man in shirt and trousers, dark and slight of build, standing near the window and looking out at the field. A convict stood near the iron bedstead. It was the hospital boy, holding a bag. After a quick glance at Ruhiton, he moved away from the bed and looked at the man near the window.

'He's here, sir,' said the Bengali warder behind Ruhiton.

The man in shirt and trousers turned around quickly from the window. He looked keenly at Ruhiton. Stepping forward he asked, 'Is your name Ruhiton Kurmi?'

Ruhiton Kurmi nodded in assent. Although he couldn't hear him clearly, he had read his lips. Astonishment flashed across the man's young eyes. Not only surprise, but also something akin to reverence spread across his face. His voice echoed the same feeling. 'I'm the doctor here, I've come to examine you.'

This was not the doctor who had accompanied the superintendent on his first day in this jail. This one was much younger. His slight build made him look very young. He didn't appear to be a doctor at all. 'Come near the window, please, sit here on the bed,' the doctor continued. 'There's more light here. It'll be easier to examine you.'

Ruhiton took a look at the staircase on the left. Then he walked up to the window and sat down on the bed. The doctor took a position near him. He scanned Ruhiton from head to toe with great concentration. Without a word, he seemed to size up Ruhiton's entire body with his eyes. At times he frowned, at other times his face tightened, his expression becoming serious. He even stood on tiptoe to examine the top of Ruhiton's head.

Ruhiton braced himself. This young lad would undoubtedly bring up whores too, just as Khelu Chowdhury had.

'This is quite an old condition. You've been suffering for a long time, haven't you?' the doctor asked.

'Yes.' Ruhiton nodded.

'How strange!' the doctor said. 'Didn't the doctor at the previous jail examine you?'

'He did,' Ruhiton answered half indifferently. 'I use the ointment he gave me on my hands and feet.'

The young doctor's face was suffused with irritation and rage. He beckoned to the convict acting as the hospital boy, taking the bag from him. Opening the bag, the doctor took out a shining piece of iron resembling a long nail and some cotton. 'Have you ever had your blood tested?' he asked.

'No.' Ruhiton shook his head.

'How long has it been since your fingers began to rot away like this?' the doctor enquired.

Ruhiton tried to remember, knitting his hairless eyebrows. He grew confused, unable to do so.

Touching Ruhiton's palm and fingers with the piece of iron, the doctor asked, 'Can you remember since when your fingers have been bent this way?'

'No.' Ruhiton shook his head again.

'Strange!' exclaimed the young doctor. 'No pain or burning sensation?'

'I don't feel any pain or anything.' Ruhiton shook his head. 'But I feel as though I have a fever at times.'

'Feel as though you have a fever? It isn't actually a fever?' the doctor asked in surprise.

'It might be,' Ruhiton said.

'You have fever now,' said the doctor. Looking at Ruhiton's feet, he asked, 'And two or three of your nails are gone, doesn't it hurt?'

'No.' Ruhiton shook his head.

The doctor was stunned into silence.

'I didn't even feel it when I lost the nails, I don't know when or how it happened,' Ruhiton said indifferently.

'Didn't even feel it?' Tapping his nails with the piece of iron, the doctor asked him, 'Can you feel this?'

'I don't feel anything even if I plunge my fingers into boiling rice. How will I feel this?' Ruhiton said in some surprise.

'You don't feel anything if you plunge your fingers into boiling rice?' The doctor stared at him in astonishment. 'What about cold water?'

'No sensation.' Ruhiton shook his head.

'It's progressed a long way then,' the doctor said. Stabbing Ruhiton's finger with the pointed tip of the piece of iron, he asked, 'Can you feel this?'

Ruhiton shook his head to indicate he couldn't.

'Shut your eyes for a bit and answer my questions,' the doctor told him.

Ruhiton looked suspiciously at the doctor. Then he shut his eyes.

Poking the bulbous growths on his hands and face with his piece of iron, the doctor asked, 'Does it hurt? Do you feel anything?'

'No.' Ruhiton shook his head.

'Fully anaesthetized,' the doctor muttered.

Ruhiton opened his eyes.

The doctor was looking at him. 'Can't you feel the mucus trickling from your nose?'

'Not always,' Ruhiton replied. He made to wipe it off with the back of his hand.

Before he could, the doctor wiped it off with the wad of cotton in his hand. Taking a piece of paper from his bag, he wrapped the cotton in it and put it away. Ruhiton watched with a mixture of surprise and curiosity.

'No more doubt, there's no more doubt,' the doctor muttered, his expression troubled.

A convict appeared and came up to the bedstead. He held an aluminium bowl with muri, chickpeas and a banana in it. In his other hand he had a glass of tea.

'What do you want?' asked the doctor.

'I've brought his breakfast, sir,' said the convict in Hindi, pointing to Ruhiton. Ruhiton looked at him.

'Your breakfast is here,' said the doctor. 'Eat up, please.'

Ruhiton accepted the bowl and the glass. Through the open door, he spotted Khelu Chowdhury in the kitchen area on the other side of the courtyard. Khelu Chowdhury and the other prisoners were looking at him. Ruhiton turned back to the doctor. An old table lay near the bed. Ruhiton put his bowl and glass on it.

'Your illness has progressed,' said the doctor. 'I have no idea why you haven't been examined all this time. You should have been treated much, much earlier. You should have been given medicines. Did anyone in your family have this illness? Have you seen any of them with it?'

'Never.' Ruhiton shook his head vehemently.

'Your grandparents or parents or wife or anyone else?' the doctor persisted.

'No. No.' Ruhiton shook his head violently again.

The doctor was flustered. 'Have your breakfast,' he said softly, looking at Ruhiton.

Popping a fistful of muri into his mouth, Ruhiton sipped his tea. The doctor handed his bag to the hospital boy. He was looking grim.

'Is it a very bad disease, doctor?' Ruhiton croaked.

The doctor tried to smile. 'All illnesses are bad. But they're all curable if treated properly. But it's been left very late in your case. You need medicine quickly.'

'How do you get this disease?' Ruhiton seemed to stop breathing as he posed his question. His eyes widened. And without his knowing it, some muri dropped down from his mouth.

'There could be many reasons,' answered the doctor. 'This isn't a dangerously contagious disease. If at all, it's children who are infected. That's why I was asking you whether your parents had it. It can also be passed on by grandparents.'

'But neither my parents nor my grandparents suffered from this disease,' Ruhiton's voice croaked hoarsely. His jaws were still moving like a cow chewing the cud, the half-chewed muri now trickling out of the corners of his mouth in a mush. 'Do bad people get this disease?' he asked.

The doctor looked probingly at Ruhiton. 'Bad people? Not at all. Even good, innocent people suffer from this illness.'

Ruhiton's inflamed, unblinking eyes were trained on the doctor. He popped in another fistful of muri, and his jaws started moving again. 'Can you get this disease from sleeping with whores at fairgrounds?' he asked plaintively.

The doctor frowned, then laughed unexpectedly. 'Oh no,' he said, 'this isn't the disease you're thinking of. Now I see why you were asking about bad people. No, this isn't an illness like that. This disease affects the surface of the skin, but it penetrates all the way to the bone, robs you of sensations. Anyone can get it. And children get it easily because it's infectious. Adults aren't usually affected if they're careful.'

'What illness is this?' Ruhiton grunted. His face, the jaws still moving and the eyes bloodshot, looked swollen.

The doctor looked serious now. Running his eyes over Ruhiton, he said, 'It's true that it's been left very late, but you'll be cured. This disease is called leprosy.'

Ruhiton's jaws stopped moving. The thickened, cracked skin on his face made it look like an ancient blood-hued slab of terracotta. 'Kut!' he said, using his dialect to refer to the disease.

'Yes, leprosy,' the doctor responded. 'The disease is not as fearsome as people think. But people are afraid of it. And it's already quite late in your case. You cannot be kept here any longer. You'll probably be taken elsewhere before lunch.'

'Elsewhere?' Ruhiton asked, worried.

'Yes, elsewhere within the jail,' the doctor said. 'Your treatment must be started without the slightest delay. I'm going to make arrangements now. Finish your breakfast.'

The young doctor's eyes and voice still held a sort of deference. Now slightly tragic. Signalling to the hospital boy, he went towards the door. Ruhiton turned to look at him. He saw Khelu Chowdhury and the others surround the doctor as soon as he went outside. Ruhiton turned away. The field stretched out before him through the window. But he could see nothing. His bloodshot, unblinking eyes reflected a wounded, perplexed question, infinite in measure. His lips moved, and silently he muttered, 'Kut! I have kut…'

Chapter Thirteen

A SEPARATE CELL had been earmarked for Ruhiton in the area for leprosy patients. He had been transferred there and his treatment had begun. Like the others, Ruhiton also moved about within the perimeter of the area for leprosy-afflicted prisoners. But he couldn't have conversations with any of them. The other prisoners with leprosy belonged to worlds that had nothing in common with his. Some of them mocked him, teased him, tried to provoke him in different ways. Ruhiton was enraged by their crude language and behaviour. Fortunately not all of them were like this. Some held Ruhiton in high esteem even though they came from different worlds. They accorded him respect. As a result, squabbles often broke out, with people taking one side or the other. There were even fistfights. The alarm bell wasn't rung when these incidents occurred. The warder and his mates threw themselves on the prisoners with their batons and belts. After both sides had received some random blows, things quietened down again.

The edict of time was absolute, however. Nothing remained unchanged in the world outside or, for that matter, inside this jail. Everything changed. Kept changing. Ruhiton knew this very well. Some of the prisoners who had tried to provoke him in the first few months had lost interest now. They no longer took any pleasure in baiting him.

He liked the young doctor. Although he was a prison doctor, his conversation and behaviour were different. He didn't seem to be treating Ruhiton merely as an act of duty. Or discharging his responsibility only because he was paid for it. Whenever he looked at Ruhiton, it always seemed to be with curiosity. And that sense of deference. Yet he never asked a question beyond the limits of his position. Nor said anything.

Once he had realized that Ruhiton was not afraid of this disease, he had told him categorically that the parts of his nose and ears which had lost all sensation, along with some parts of his fingers and toes, would never be restored. Some permanent marks would remain on his forehead, cheek, chin, ankles, and elbows. But he had planted a question in Ruhiton's mind. 'Try to remember whether you used to visit anyone with leprosy when you were a child,' he kept repeating. 'Someone who would hug you, hold you in their arms, maybe your nose was running. Children don't realize when their noses run. Leprosy germs can take that route into a person's body. If there are sores or wounds on the skin, or insect bites, the germs can enter that way too. Try to remember. You must have been near a leprosy patient at some time or the other. Maybe you had wounds or sores on your skin at the time.'

'Maybe I was poisoned with this disease through my meals in jail,' Ruhiton had said one day, airing his suspicion.

Laughing uproariously, the young doctor had said, 'Oh no, nothing like that. This is a skin disease, it can't come from anything you eat. And if that were the case, they could have given you much more lethal poison. Besides, why would they poison you alone, they could have poisoned everyone from your party. It's no use thinking along these lines.'

Ruhiton had accepted the doctor's argument. To begin with, it was very difficult not to believe him. Besides, why would people who could easily get rid of him whenever they wanted to, take such a roundabout route?

For the first time in all his years in jail, he had been separated from his mates. Initially, except during interrogation, he had been kept in seclusion but close to them. A few years later, they had more or less allowed people from the same party to stay together. Of course, the prisoners had had to go on fasts and strikes for this.

Ruhiton was trying to dissect his past. It was like a search for husks amidst a pile of clean, fresh rice. But he hadn't succeeded in unearthing even a single victim of leprosy. This solitary life, separated from his friends in the party, was as dim as deepening dusk. Only his past seemed bathed in bright sunlight. Especially the period when they had planned to encircle cities with villages. As part of that, they had begun to build a Liberated Zone of their own, free of enemies. You could call it full-fledged war.

The landowners and traders had become furious at the arrogance of the poor and the landless. So furious that they had singled out targets of their own accord and started killing them. Mohan Chhetri, Ruknuddin Ahmed, Shanilal, even Shuku Pongani, had begun to move around with guns. Ruhiton had got himself a gun licence too. Every landowner and trader, small or large, had had a gun. They had been given arms to keep robbers at bay. Members of the ferocious Murang tribe from Nepal used to attack them in autumn and winter. They used guns and daggers and large sickles. But those attacks took place once or twice, at specific times of the year. That was the reason the border police and army authorities maintained camps round the year at Naxalbari, Raniganj, Panighat, Mirik, and Tanglu. In reality, the landowners and traders used their guns more on the impoverished sharecroppers and tenant farmers. Besides, there was poaching in the Khashmahal area and the reserved forests.

Ruhiton and his group had not relinquished a single one of their guns. They had snatched guns from every landowner and trader in the huge area between Tukariajhar in the south and east, the Mechi in the north, and the Dalkajhar forest in the north.

And Barka Chhetri. The formidable son of the large landowner Mohan Chhetri. Yes, Ruhiton and he had remained friends well after his wedding. Did his heart skip a beat at the thought? Not at all. He had drenched the crazed, notorious murderer in blood with bare-handed blows. Yet Barka had been his childhood friend. Ruhiton would carry a bow and arrows. Barka would carry a gun. The gun was probably heavier than him. But he could lift it with ease and, supporting the butt with this chest, squeeze the trigger. How good his aim was! He wouldn't miss even by a whisker. Ruhiton's own aim with the bow and arrow wasn't bad either. They had hunted plenty of big game.

They had killed tigers, deer, and pythons. Not to mention peacocks, roosters, and rabbits. Peacocks were rare in the jungles of the Terai. Ruhiton had often shot down flying wild roosters with his bow and arrow, more often than Barka had with his gun. And that golden leopard cat? Ruhiton had shot it with an arrow and captured it alive. Barka had taken it home as a pet. But he hadn't managed to keep the beautiful creature alive very long. They went trout fishing together in the Mechi as well. Sometimes they went to the Balashon, even all the way to the Tista in the west. Besides, there was always the fishing in the mountain streams flowing out of the waterfalls, or in the lakes. Also, hunting of fish-eating wildcats.

At that time, in Ruhiton's youth, the forest department had not been very strict about enforcing hunting laws. Besides, the landowners and the forest department babus perpetually scratched each other's backs and avoided fights over hunting. The Englishmen at the tea estates used to hunt with impunity too.

Every time Ruhiton thought of Barka he was reminded of what Khelu babu had said. Oh yes, you're right, Khelu babu, Barka Chhetri was my friend. We used to go to the fairs together. We used to listen to the songs and the music. Yes, we used to gamble too. I got married. Soon afterwards, so did he. His father had actually got his eldest son a bride from Nepal. His wife's name was Maya. Mine was Mangala, his was Maya. We used to take our wives to the fairs together. We would listen to music, watch the bioscope, gamble, and drink. And our wives would hurry us back home. Those were happy days for us when we were young.

Yes, Barka's larder was full. Not mine. We would go out hunting at night. We never worried about running into a herd of elephants, or having a leopard pounce on us from a tree. He would be well fed. I wouldn't always. If Barka got to know, he would sometimes get me some food from home. But whores? On Barka's money? I am a Kurmi Mahato, Khelu babu. You've seen many Santhals, Kurmis, Oraons, and Mundas on the tea estates. We never pay to sleep with our women. Don't you know people actually want to buy our poor, deprived women?

Chapter Fourteen

BUT BARKA WAS Mohan Chhetri's son. Once he had realized that Ruhiton belonged to a different world, he had ended their friendship. He stopped spending time with Ruhiton; he even began to threaten him. Suspicious of Ruhiton and his group, he had taken to carrying his gun.

One day he had begun beating up Gobra Santhal with the butt of his gun, in Ruhiton's presence. Gobra used to be a labourer on Barka's family farm, a servant in his home. Barka had suspected Gobra of joining the group intent on killing landowners. He was beating him to make him talk. Beat? What he was doing wasn't beating. He seemed intent on killing him. Barka had blood on his hands already. Once he considered someone an enemy, he had no qualms about killing him.

Diba babu had not personally instructed Ruhiton to kill Barka. Ruhiton had attacked Barka on his own. Yes, it was true that Barka had been surprised. He had not expected to be attacked by Ruhiton. Then, breaking into a fury, he had tried to cock his gun and fire. Ruhiton had not allowed that to happen. He had known that once Barka had his gun in position, there would be no escape. So, with all his strength he had grabbed the gun first and thrown it away. Gobra Santhal had picked the gun up. Ruhiton had begun to hit Barka. As he hit him…No, his heart didn't leap into his mouth when he recalled all this, as he was doing now.

During their revolution, Gobra Santhal had laid siege to Mohan Chhetri's two-storeyed tin-roofed wooden farmhouse with a group of people. Old man Mohan Chhetri had died, along with his two sons. The work for the enemy-free Liberated Zone had begun.

Was Barka his friend? Yes, Barka had been his friend. And then his enemy. Life was like that. If every creature on earth had its own principles, so did the landless cultivator Ruhiton Kurmi. The enemy could be dealt with in only one way under those principles. Kill, or be killed.

The landowners were mainly Bengali Hindus, some Bihari Muslims, and a handful of Nepalis. The traders were mostly Marwaris. They owned all the shops, godowns, and high interest moneylending businesses. They were also gradually becoming the owners of the tea estates. Their paw prints were everywhere—from the tea gardens to the forests and agricultural resources of the Terai. These traders and landowners were the targets of the first wave of attacks when Ruhiton and his group were creating their Liberated Zone. Many of them had escaped with their lives to Siliguri. Those who had wanted to fight, like Barka, had had the fight taken out of them forever. The border police and the army had not been prepared for this unexpected armed uprising. Not surprisingly, their forces had initially scattered in different directions. Later, they had quickly mounted a counter-attack by surrounding the hills in the northwest from the southern plains of Siliguri and the Bihar border.

But the soldiers of the uprising had been unable to put up a resistance to the thugs and vultures from the cities. Just as vultures swoop down on the corpse after being intimated by flies that a cow has died, these ruffians too had pounced. Taking advantage of the uprising, they had looted goods worth lakhs of rupees in their trucks. None of the revolutionaries had had any experience of how things turn out after an uprising. And those thugs and hoodlums, many of them disguised as members of political parties, were poised to exploit any situation.

Ruhiton could not forget the incredible enthusiasm and courage of the people in every village in the Terai. He had personally toured all the villages and habitations. From boys to old men, from men to women, everyone had seemed transformed. Had they really gained a new life? Many of them had even given up drinking and beating their wives. Unlike many others, Ruhiton was not in the habit of taking out his frustrations on his wife by beating her. Did that mean he had never beaten her up? But yes, he too had been beaten up by Mangala once or twice. Was there a Kurmi Mahato in the world who had not received a few blows from his wife after a grievous crime? At least to rid them of their drunkenness? Especially if the man had got drunk on hooch exchanged for the family's food, which he had stolen? But when Ruhiton had stopped drinking, his mother had questioned his decision, asking how this could be allowed. For Santhals and Kurmis and Mundas and Mahatos, to not drink deyong was to go against their principles.

We still have a Karam puja, we pray for Marangburu's grace, he was the one who had given deyong to the people. We still go to the Shirua—rolling in the mud—and Kisua—hunting—festivals of the Rajvanshis. This was what his mother would say. Mangala would agree. But a different wind was blowing through the Liberated Zone created by Ruhiton and his group. There was no ban on deyong or instruction about other things. Still a wave of change had swept over everyone. Everyone had become self-aware and disciplined. Disciplined, because they had become keen on performing their duty with dedication. They guarded the Liberated Zone like sentries who never slept.

What about Mangala? His wife? Despite being a Mahato, heart and soul, she had protested vehemently against the burning of a suspected witch in the Liberated Zone. No one had expected her to. Like the Karam puja and Marangburu, she used to believe in burning witches too. Which was expected. She had had several arguments with Ruhiton about this earlier. A woman who had the ability to cast a spell from a distance to suck out all the milk from a cow's teats, who could drink the blood of a baby in its mother's arms, who could set fire to a harvest—how could such a woman possibly be spared from being burnt alive? But Mangala had shown she could be. She had led the protest herself. And everyone had come to know her because of this. Oh yes, wasn't Mangala the wife of the revolutionary leader Ruhiton Kurmi? Get out, you witch doctors and exorcists.

Ruhiton was helpless. The memories kept rushing back. Whenever he remembered these things, sick and alone in jail, he wished desperately for more. Just as the baby comes to life at its mother's smell, Mangala used to have the same effect on him with hers. Even after all these years, he could never mistake that smell. Was this not a weakness in Ruhiton Kurmi's life now? His heart ached with desire to see Budhua, Karma, and Dudhi. Sometimes his heart leapt in anxiety, what if his blind mother had slipped on the loose pebbles near the waterfall and fallen in?

He was Ruhiton Kurmi, from Chunilal village in the Terai. Why should he be thinking of such things? Was it right for him to be anxious about his family? Like the rotten branches of trees, parts of his body were falling off. The rest of his body was rediscovering sensation. He could feel things again physically. He realized that he was recovering. The weakness in his nerves and bones was ebbing away. But the mission of his life now was not simply to overcome his illness. He was still in jail—secluded, sick, alone. Why did his breath stop at times with anxiety for his wife, his children, his mother? Why, for that matter, did the doctor's words keep coming back?

'Don't imagine your life has ended with this illness. You will recover. You will still be able to have children when you go back home to your wife. Yes, you will have healthy children, free of diseases, just like before.'

Really? Really! But why did the doctor tell him all this?

'Do you understand what listening to all this does to me, Mangli? Which part of my heart does it all go into? And wherever it goes, where does it want to drive my heart? But I am Ruhiton Kurmi. Ruhiton Kurmi.'

At once he remembered that he was a 'fanla' Bhumij. The Santhal and Munda girls used the word to describe a lover who cheated, a scoundrel. Mangala addressed him this way sometimes. It was actually an endearment.

But Ruhiton didn't want to remember all this. He didn't want to ask why this disease had taken root in his body. For asking this was an unnecessary weakness too. He desperately scoured the list of every person he had met in the life he had left behind. To identify, as the doctor had said, the person who had passed on this disease to him.

But the more the days went by, the more this question retreated from his mind. How would it help, anyway, to remember who it might have been? Instead, he frequently felt a sharp urge, an urgent curiosity, to find out what the Liberated Zone was like now. He had heard different things from people in jail. He didn't know how true they were, but all of the versions spelt hopelessness and failure. He didn't wish to hear this. He felt a constant surge of anxiety. How was everyone? Death, injuries, looting, arson in some cases, stockpiling of arms—all of this was true. None of it was a lie. All this had taken place, to create a new world. Ruhiton didn't deny it. But he never wished to hear that the people from his party in that area were nothing but murderers, robbers, and criminals.

Chapter Fifteen

A YEAR AND some months passed in the leprosy ward in the jail in Calcutta. The original doctor had not visited for several months. A new doctor visited him now. This one spoke and behaved differently. 'I don't know,' was his only answer whenever Ruhiton asked him about the previous doctor. Human beings considered many things strange, but there was nothing stranger in the world than human beings, mused Ruhiton.

But ever since the previous doctor had stopped visiting him, a thought had begun to flash in his mind. Not a thought, but a face. He used to work on Shanilal's land. His name was Perwa. No one knew why his parents had given him that name, or whether it had been given someone else. Perwa referred to paayra—pigeon. He was from a family of cultivators who had moved from a tea estate. Perwa had been a close friend of his, a constant companion particularly during the time they were creating their Liberated Zone. Perwa had always regretted allowing Shanilal to hoodwink him and escape with his belongings. And when their free zone was attacked, Perwa had died in the firing.

Perwa's face glinted like a needle amidst a mound of pebbles before Ruhiton's eyes. Red bulbous sores had erupted on Perwa's face a few months before his death. His nose, ears, eyebrows and the skin on his face had changed in appearance too. Perwa did use an ointment for ringworm. Ruhiton hadn't had the time then to observe all this closely although Perwa and he used to be together most of the time.

There were no more wounds left on Ruhiton's body. But almost none of his toes were left. More than half of his fingers had withered. He would never have nails again in this lifetime. The tip of his nose was completely flattened. His nostrils had been virtually replaced by two openings above his lips, covered by a thin layer of skin. Fresh patches of skin had appeared on his hands and feet, and especially on his face, under his eyes, and on his cheeks and forehead. They looked pink, like the new skin that grows over a wound. His eyelids were as red and as devoid of lashes as before. No hair had grown on his eyebrows. His scalp was bare, shining. Both his earlobes had fallen off. The thick little sticks no longer ran through the holes in his ear that his mother had made for him when he was a child.

Ruhiton saw Perwa in his own hands and feet these days. He felt the urge to say this to his old doctor. But there was no sign of him. The young doctor hadn't told him he would no longer be visiting him. No matter, he was no longer angry with the person who had passed on this disease to him. On the contrary, he felt saddened at the thought that he would never see Perwa again.

Ruhiton's cough had worsened of late. He felt feeble after a coughing fit. The doctor here didn't reveal much.

One day he was suddenly loaded into a van outside the jail, surrounded by armed guards, as before. Only the officer who used to offer him cigarettes and chatter away wasn't there. Ruhiton didn't smoke any more, however. It made him cough, hurt his chest.

Ruhiton did not have to go on a long journey from the jail in the van. He was taken into a building. It looked like a hospital. His chest was photographed in a room. What they call an X-ray. He was brought back to the jail immediately afterwards. And exactly seven days after this incident, shortly after lunch, a jail officer arrived. Who knew what sort of officer he was. He wasn't dressed in any kind of uniform. Ruhiton thought it must be someone junior to the jailer. He was accompanied by a warder. The plainclothes officer made the warder unlock Ruhiton's cell. Then he told Ruhiton to change from his convict's outfit into his own clothes from his tin trunk.

Ruhiton knew that questions or protests would be in vain. Maybe some new phase was about to begin. He put on his pyjamas and striped red shirt. He no longer used his rubber sandals. He could neither slip his toeless feet into the sandals, nor walk in them. Ruhiton saw that the warder had picked up his trunk unbidden, saying, 'Please come along.'

Where? The question was pointless. But now dressed in his own clothes after eight years and a few months, he appeared unfamiliar to himself. It all appeared quite novel to him. As soon as he emerged in his own pyjamas and shirt, the prisoners in the leprosy ward all bade him farewell with different cries and in different languages, their arms raised. What did all this mean? Not all the older patients were still there. Several had left, others had arrived. Ruhiton raised his arm in farewell too.

His gait had changed completely now. Not just because of the cracked bone above his rectum. Because of his non-existent toes, he had to curl the front half of his foot to grip the ground. It made his arms swing exaggeratedly. And he had to walk very slowly, practically hobbling.

Ruhiton arrived at the jail office with the plainclothes officer and the warder. 'Khelu babu and the others had implored me to arrange a meeting with them,' the jailer said as soon as he saw him. 'But my orders won't permit it. I had told them that Ruhiton Kurmi has been released. Besides, we don't have time. Here's your train ticket. It's for a three-tier coach.

You can sleep on the way.' About to hand over a packet with two tickets in them, he put them in Ruhiton's breast pocket instead. 'Just a minute,' he continued, 'we need one or two thumb impressions. But...' Pausing suddenly, the jailer turned to the plainclothes officer to ask in surprise, 'How do I get a thumb impression from Ruhiton Kurmi, Mr Majumdar? Where is his thumb?'

Walking up to the desk to examine a ledger, Mr Majumdar said gravely, 'Take an impression of whichever finger is still intact. Why bother to ask? Besides, this isn't a particularly important issue.'

A single word kept ringing in Ruhiton's breast, release. Release? Where would he go? What kind of release was this? He had never thought of release, never sought it either. He wasn't prepared for it.

'Sit down, here, sit on this chair,' said the plainclothes officer, coming up to him. 'The Darjeeling Mail leaves from Sealdah station every evening. I will take you to Sealdah. If you show them your ticket, the railway people will show you where to sit in the train. The train will stop at New Jalpaiguri. You'll have to take the bus there. Travelling all the way by train will be very difficult. You'll have to get off at Kishenganj, change trains, and travel to Galgalia from Purnea. All this boarding and disembarking will be hard for you. You'll get a bus in Siliguri. You'll just have to ask someone. Keep this money for your bus fare and expenses on the way.' When he had finished, the officer tucked some money into his pocket, just as the jailer had.

By bus from Siliguri? To Chunilal village? This meant he really was being released. And had Khelu babu and the rest wanted to meet him because they had got the news? Ruhiton's heart and head were no longer working. He could feel neither pleasure nor joy. Only his withered hands and feet seemed to be trembling in excitement. He had never imagined such a day would come. He had never imagined being released. The whole thing appeared extraordinary. The undeniable reality that he was Ruhiton Kurmi seemed to have become unreal. Ruhiton Kurmi released! But indeed he had a train ticket in his pocket, and even travelling expenses. But was he really going back to that old tract of land in the Terai? Where… where Mangala and his children were—their Liberated Zone! Beads of perspiration gathered on Ruhiton's face. He had stopped sweating during the illness. Especially on his hands and feet and face. He was sweating now. His mind was in turmoil, though he couldn't identify why.

Chapter Sixteen

THIS WAS THE Kharibari region if you defined it by the jurisdiction of police stations. The New Jalpaiguri station was new to Ruhiton. He was familiar with Siliguri station. But he had to take the bus from New Jalpaiguri. From there the road ran through Siliguri, turning east at the Matigara Tea Estate. The Terai railway line ran alongside.

All these roads were familiar, at his fingertips. But the town of Siliguri had changed beyond recognition. Everything had changed so much over the past eight and a half years that Ruhiton was befuddled. He had not been able to recognize many of the places. Not a single person had recognized him on the way. One of the railway employees with a list in his hand had said his name out aloud twice in the train at Sealdah station. Some people had even turned to look at him, looking away indifferently the next moment.

Ruhiton would never have been able to board the bus amidst the crowds at New Jalpaiguri. He had not even been able to identify which of the buses would go towards his home in the southeast. Both tasks had been beyond him. But a complete stranger had come up to him to ask where he was going. Ruhiton had been somewhat astonished. He didn't know the man, but his manner of asking the question had appeared familiar. He was the one who had pointed out the correct bus.

Ruhiton had had to move around with his tin trunk on his shoulder. He had tried to hold it in his hand from time to time. It was very difficult. He couldn't curl his fingers around the handle. Nevertheless, he had slipped the remnants of his fingers under the handle so that the trunk could dangle from his palm. He hadn't been able to hold it this way very long.

No one in the bus had recognized Ruhiton. Nor had he spotted a familiar face. It wasn't supposed to have been this way. As soon as the bus had left the town to enter the countryside, he had more or less been able to recognize the places they had passed through. He had found a place to sit in the bus. Even a place for his trunk. He had recognized each of the tea estates on the way, along with the roads leading into them. The Bagdogra, Singhijhora, Krishnapur, and Atal tea estates were quite some distance to the east of the Matigara Tea Estate. After Atal, the road descended to the south, towards Naxalbari. Passing the small tea estate in the southern Terai, it went on towards the village and the farms. He had had to get off near the South Terai Tea Estate. He had noticed something new along the way. Frequent police checkposts, tents, and military camps. They were far more numerous than before. What did this mean? All the news of failure that he had received about the Liberated Zone must be horrifyingly true. But what did it mean that he had not yet come across a single familiar face? He knew very well why no one seemed to recognize him. Even if the thought made his heart heavy, what choice did he have but to accept the reason? It wasn't just his face, his entire appearance had changed.

It wasn't as though his problems had begun only when he had got off at New Jalpaiguri station. They had started the previous day, in jail. His reasoning, his thoughts, his feelings no longer seemed to be functioning properly. He was shaking inwardly in excitement and this was slowing him down.

The day was well advanced by the time he reached Naxalbari. Some of the passengers mentioned Ramdhan village as soon as they had passed the South Terai Tea Estate. Ruhiton's heart began to thump uncomfortably in excitement. And yet he didn't know any of the people who had mentioned the village. He had to get off soon after the large tea estate of the South Terai Company. The rest of the distance could be covered by foot, through the farm.

The place where Ruhiton got off no longer looked as it once did. It was crowded with shops and people now. To the north, the mountain rose against the sky. Mirik, Sukiapokhri, Darjeeling, Pulbazar. There were hidden trails through the jungles of the Terai to the top of the hills. Many local people travelled that way. The border of the Liberated Zone was a little to the north. But the first thing he saw were two policemen in uniform. They were standing on one side of the road, laughing and talking, a cycle balanced between them. They didn't look like ordinary constables, they must be inspectors. They looked once or twice at Ruhiton. Their eyes were blank. Everyone around appeared indifferent too, most of them didn't even throw him a glance. The entire picture seemed to convey to Ruhiton that the Liberated Zone, indeed, no longer existed.

Here too, an incident similar to the one in New Jalpaiguri took place. Munching on a paan, a Bengali man in a dhoti and kurta came up to him to ask where he wanted to go. Ruhiton named his destination. To his surprise, the man smiled, then pointed out the way with his finger before disappearing. Ruhiton didn't remember ever having seen him before. Who was he? And how strange that he couldn't see one familiar face here either. Except for a single old man. It was the Marwari seth, Deora. He was sitting on a gaddi in the big grocery. Their enormous godown was next door. The man had escaped with his life during the uprising.

Ruhiton began to walk along his route. It would take a long time, for he would have to walk very slowly, his lower abdomen thrust forward, gripping the ground with his toeless feet.

The path that Ruhiton was walking along used to have dense jungles on both sides earlier. They had been cleared. He kept encountering new houses on the way. These were not exactly ordinary farmers' or labourers' homes. Who knew who the owners were! The tall, shiny buildings on wooden platforms made it clear that rich people lived in this area now. Ruhiton wasn't the only one walking along this road; there were others too. They looked very familiar. But he didn't actually know any of them. Or maybe it was just that he couldn't recognize them. For he still could not accept any of this as real. His release from jail. His taking the train, then the bus from Siliguri, and, now, going home. He was Ruhiton Kurmi. Only someone possessed by a demon could accept all this. A long time ago, Ruhiton might have believed all of it. But he had long lost faith in possession by a demon. Just as Mangala had stopped believing in witches. Mangala! Mangli!

No, Ruhiton could no longer deny the truth that he had been released from the jail in Calcutta and had returned to Chunilal village. Not just the village, he was actually almost home now. And as soon as he thought of Mangala, his excitement began to quicken. It also prevented him from sizing up the actual situation. But he still couldn't quite grasp that he was free and returning home.

The further Ruhiton progressed, the thicker the jungle around him became. He took comfort from this. This was the environment he was familiar with. Sal, cotton trees, rain trees, Indian redwoods—a crowd of enormous trees. Farmland could be seen through gaps in the forest, low walls of earth around them to dam the flow from the waterfalls. This wasn't the time for the Aman crop. Nor for the Boro crop; this was the season prior to that. Still, the fields were almost completely green. The Ravi crop had been harvested earlier. Pumpkins were growing in some of the fields. He had heard of other varieties of rice being introduced. Maybe some of those were growing now. The crops seemed to be ripening.

But what was this? Ruhiton stopped abruptly. A building that looked like an office bungalow stood in the shade of the forest—a sparkling red bungalow. A man in police uniform stood near the gate. Had a new police station come up here in the interiors? Hearing a cycle bell and conversation behind him, he turned around to see the two men in khaki uniform he had spotted earlier. The paan-munching man in the dhoti and kurta was there as well. Were they following him?

Ruhiton no longer expected to see remnants of the Liberated Zone. Through the gaps in the dense jungle it appeared that the sunlight was receding towards Siliguri. Were shadows gathering over the Mechi? Was a cold wind descending from the mountain? The sky above the peaks was clear, but it was never a clear blue at this time of day. It was usually streaked with grey. Yet there was a faint red glow every now and then in the Darjeeling sky to the north. It probably came from the snow-capped peak in the distance. The chirping of the crickets was becoming louder. Ruhiton was perspiring. He was tired.

Chapter Seventeen

'RUHITON KURMI, ISN'T it? It's me, we've met before.'

Ruhiton stopped abruptly on hearing this. Someone had spoken in a tongue similar to the Madesia dialect. Different kinds of dialects were used here—the Santhals, Bhumijs, Mundas, Kurmis, Oraons used their own respective languages within their clans. Just as the Nepalis or the Rajvanshi Kshatriyas did when talking to one another. Besides these, there was also a mixed tongue. This was the one everyone used in general. The Adivasis here were said to be Paschimas—from the west. So were Hindi speakers. Only Marwaris were referred to as Marwari or sethji.

Ruhiton realized that a small crowd of people had gathered. They stared at him with curiosity in their eyes; some appeared astonished, while some were smiling. Ruhiton knew the spot they were gathered at. This was where the ritual community puja for the goddess Kali was conducted. It looked a little different now. A small shed with a roof but no walls had come up beneath the tree. But who were these people? The bearded man in the lungi and kurta looked extremely familiar. It was he who approached Ruhiton with a smile. 'Do you recognize me?' he asked. 'I recognized you right away, mind you. Not that there's any way to recognize you. But then this disease is Allah's gift to you, what can you do.'

So the news of his arrival had preceded him. Was this Ruknuddin Ahmed's brother Kachimuddin? Ruknuddin had been killed by Ruhiton's party. Ruhiton didn't remember now whether he had a son or not. But he had a brother, whom Ruhiton used to know. His name was Kachimuddin. Yes, this was the man. He had escaped from Mirik's Khashmahal to Darjeeling. Kachimuddin was an educated man with contacts everywhere. He had been on friendly terms with senior police officers, top leaders, wealthy tea estate owners, and businessmen. Ruknuddin used to depend on him a lot.

'We've come to receive you, Ruhiton. Give me your trunk now, you needn't carry it any more.' Practically snatching the trunk out of Ruhiton's hand, he looked over his shoulder to say, 'Take this, one of you.'

A strongly built young man in nothing but a loincloth ran up at once to take the trunk.

'Now tell me, do you recognize me?' Kachimuddin repeated.

For the first time, Ruhiton realized that his own voice had turned nasal. 'Kachimuddin…' he said hesitantly.

'Right you are,' Kachimuddin burst out. 'We're old-timers, after all. How would you not recognize us?' He put an arm round Ruhiton's shoulder.

Ruhiton's shoulder stiffened. Was Kachimuddin welcoming him with an arm round his shoulders? What were all these tricks that reality was playing on him?

'Then you recognize me too?' asked someone else, running up to him.

It was a well-built young man in a shirt, his dhoti drawn up above his knees. The regional accent of the Rajvanshis was evident. Ruhiton could not recognize him.

'But this is Baralal,' Kachimuddin explained. 'Shanilal's son.'

Baralal, meaning Barahalal. He had been so young. He was grown up now. Shanilal had survived, Ruhiton thought to himself. He must be living in great comfort now. Where had the Liberated Zone gone and who were these people in whose midst he had arrived?

Turning around, Kachimuddin raised his arm and called out loudly, 'What's the matter? Come along, Dil Narayan babu. Why are you hanging back, Achhalal? Come on, Narsing Chhetri. But where are Ruhiton's sons? Budhua and Karma! Come to your father.'

Ruhiton felt his heart beating so fast he actually thought he would stop breathing. Budhua and Karma! Where were they? The crowd surged forward. But he could not identify Budhua and Karma among them. The ninth year now. That was how long he hadn't seen them. How much had they grown, what did they look like, he had no idea. They hadn't been killed, then. Deep in his heart he had harboured the anxiety that his family was no longer alive, that they had probably all died. Yet, even after discovering that his sons were alive, Ruhiton was unable to feel relief or happiness. Nothing seemed real to him.

'Here, Budhua, Karma.' Kachimuddin led two strapping young men by their hands to him. 'Go to your father.'

Ruhiton looked at Budhua and Karma. He could recognize them now. They didn't resemble each other. The differences had sharpened as they had grown. But he recognized them. Budhua had taken after Mangala, and Karma after him. Karma looked as though he was older. He was taller and broader than Budhua. But although they were the sons of a Kurmi and a Mahato, this wasn't evident from their appearance. Like Barka Chhetri, they were dressed in trousers and half-sleeved shirts. Both had rubber slippers on their feet. Their hair was heavily oiled and slicked down. Budhua had a watch on his left wrist. Both were staring at Ruhiton. They didn't take a single step forward towards him. Their eyes were blank, as though they didn't recognize Ruhiton. As though they were seeing a stranger. And their faces looked solemn and uncomfortable.

Ruhiton realized it must be difficult for his sons to recognize him. Naturally. Love welled up in his heart. Was this how fathers felt? Did a dam burst in the heart on seeing one's children after a long time? But how stiffly they stood. They showed no sign of coming up to him. Should he be the one to go up to them, to touch them?

Ruhiton couldn't bring himself to do this. It wasn't possible to take anyone's hand after all these years, with no contact, no communication all this time, and especially if they looked so solemn, so stiff. Not even if they were one's own children. Their expressions were stern, they refused to look at him directly. Their clothes, watch, and appearance were different too. But still, what a surprise!

Ruhiton smiled. He looked at his sons with a smile. His eyes asked silently, 'How's your mother? She's alive, isn't she? And my blind old mother? And Dudhi? My lovely daughter?'

'We got the news of your arrival yesterday,' Kachimuddin said. 'The inspector at the new police camp told us that you were coming back. We decided on the spot to meet you here and take you home.'

Ruhiton noticed that virtually none of the simple, poor people had come. He didn't know the people who had gathered. It was true that many years had passed. But did time have no consideration at all? Did it have to turn everything into a lie, make it unreal? Despite all the changes, Ruhiton could sense that none of these people belonged to his world. Dil Narayan, Achhalal, Narsingh Chhetri—all seemed to be traders or landowners.

'Come along, Ruhiton, there's no need to wait here any longer.' Kachimuddin pulled him gently by the arm. 'Come along home.'

Ruhiton walked with them on his toeless feet. A few children ran on ahead, shouting. A couple of dogs barked.

Chapter Eighteen

RUHITON STOPPED ABRUPTLY on seeing the house from his father's time. There used to be a slight slope on the west. It had been levelled off with earth. But now the ground dipped to the west again. Like an old man with a damaged hip. But the roof of the eastern portion had been rethatched with fresh grass. And a plump cow was tied to the post. She, too, looked at Ruhiton when she spotted the crowd of people. As though Mangala herself had raised her eyes to look at him.

'Why did you stop here?' Narsingh Chhetri spoke in the mixed tongue. 'Do you think this is your home?' He laughed.

Everyone else laughed with him. Ruhiton was surprised. What was so funny? Why should he not recognize his own home? Yes, he had been suffering from a serious illness. His condition was similar to that of a tree battered by a storm. The branches and leaves that had fallen off would not grow back. But he was alive, after all. Every inch of his skin was sensitive now, every part of his body perspired. He was a little hard of hearing. But his eyesight was as good as ever; he could see everything clearly. His voice had become nasal, because a bone in the centre had wasted away and all but disappeared. But it wasn't hoarse as it once was.

'How would he know?' said the man named Dil Narayan. 'Everything has changed, but he had no way of knowing, did he? He had no contact with his family, they weren't allowed to go and see him in jail. As far as I know, they didn't exchange letters.'

Letters. That had simply not been possible. Neither he nor Mangala knew how to read or write in any language.

'Listen, Ruhiton, this isn't your house any more,' said Kachimuddin. 'That one is.' He pointed to a wooden building standing on a platform of wood to the east.

Ruhiton looked in that direction in surprise. The wood and the tin roof were painted black. The floor of wooden planks stood on thick stumps of sal. It was practically like a landowner's or a trader's house. Houses such as these were not damaged easily by floodwater. A wooden staircase rose upstairs like a ladder. The front portion of the first floor was uncovered, like a veranda. It was almost like Mohan Chhetri's house, where the granary of the Liberated Zone had been set up. Corn had been planted in the fields in front of and around the house. A few women stood there, looking in his direction.

'Come.' Once again it was Kachimuddin who led him by the hand. 'The government gave your family land to cultivate. They paid for the new house too. Your old house was washed away by the floods three or four years ago. Come along.' He led Ruhiton towards the new building.

The government had provided land to cultivate, built a new house! For Ruhiton Kurmi's family?

Kachimuddin was still talking. 'Whatever may have happened, you are Ruhiton Kurmi. The government cannot be unfair to you. Times have changed, you know. The government is trying to give land to many others like you. But your case is different. You are Ruhiton Kurmi. Our party, even government officers, have been instructed to ensure that your family does not suffer.'

He was Ruhiton Kurmi, Ruhiton thought to himself. But was he the same Ruhiton Kurmi? Even his own name seemed out of place. He walked through the corn fields with everyone else and stopped in front of the house. The crowd surrounded him on all sides.

'Where are you, Budhua?' Kachimuddin bellowed. 'Call your mother. Tell her to bring your wife too.'

The group of women visible from a distance earlier were nowhere to be seen now. A wooden wall ran next to the wooden staircase, taking a turn to the right. A bench was laid out in front. Next to the bench was another small room on four thick posts of sal. It was like the rooms used by landowners to store their grain. A cycle leant against a post near the room.

'My mother? Where is she?' Ruhiton looked around and asked a question for the first time, without addressing anyone in particular.

'She died a long time ago,' answered Shanilal's son Barahalal. 'Two years after all the killing.'

The killing? Was Barahalal referring to the creation of the Liberated Zone? Even as he was asking himself this question, a figure appeared near the wall on the right and came towards him. Ruhiton felt as though his heart were struck by lightning. Mangala! It *was* Mangli, wasn't it? But was this also a trick played by the demon? She seemed to have grown younger. There was a reddish-brown gash of sindoor in her hair and a teep on her forehead. Her hair was combed tightly and tied up. Silver bangles on her arms. Were they really silver? She was dressed in a mill-made sari with a red border. Something was shining on her nose too. She was looking at him gravely just like his sons had; her eyes appeared surprised and unfamiliar. She seemed not to recognize Ruhiton. She looked him up and down. There seemed to be fear in her eyes.

Ruhiton was shaken, his excitement dampening. His mother had died; Mangala was staring at him with apprehension and surprise. Should he weep, or should he smile at Mangala? The torrents were flowing freely in his heart. Would Mangala keep her distance too? The sight of her was making his heart murmur. Surely she hadn't married again?

A girl of thirteen or fourteen with a shy expression and wide eyes came up and stood beside Mangala. Mangala looked at Ruhiton. Then she said, pointing to the girl, 'Budhua's wife.'

His son's wife. Ruhiton's red, lashless eyelids became moist. But he smiled in silence. Budhua's young wife slipped away after a single look at Ruhiton. She was embarrassed. Naturally.

'Dudhi? Where's Dudhi?' Ruhiton asked in his nasal voice.

There wasn't even a ghost of a smile on Mangala's face. 'She got married two months ago,' she answered. 'She lives in Balaijhora, at the tea estate.' With a quick glance at the rest of the people, she slipped away too.

'Sit down now,' said Kachimuddin, helping Ruhiton to sit down on the bench. 'Talk to your family. We'll come again later.' Signalling to the crowd to leave, he snapped at some children nearby, 'And what are all of you gaping at? Get out of here.' He added loudly before leaving, 'We're leaving, Budhua. We'll be back tomorrow.'

The crowd vanished from Ruhiton's sight. And the shadows of the afternoon darkened too. A few hens and chicks milled around Ruhiton's feet. Some of them even jumped on him. A dog near the wooden staircase wagged its tail at him suspiciously. The scene suggested a more or less affluent household. Whom did the cycle belong to? Did Budhua and Karma own a cycle now? Was all of this government aid?

Ruhiton raised his eyes at a sudden flurry of movement among the chickens; he saw that Mangala had arrived. She was holding a wicker bowl. She offered it to him. Accepting the bowl, Ruhiton saw it was full of fried kernels of corn. Like a basket of white flowers. Ruhiton suddenly realized he was ravenous. But the impudent chicks were particularly greedy.

Although their tiny mouths were too small for the corn, they pounced on the bowl.

'Should I bring you some tea?' Mangala asked.

'Yes, I'll have some.' Ruhiton nodded. 'Everything has changed somehow, hasn't it, Mangli? And how are you—'

Mangala turned and vanished before Ruhiton could finish what he was saying. He looked after her with reddened eyes. He continued to stare in the direction in which she had disappeared. Darkness was descending rapidly. Indistinct voices could be heard somewhere out of sight.

Turning back, Ruhiton tried to scoop up some corn. Some of it spilled out, some stayed in his paw. He put them in his mouth quickly. The chicks scuttled about with the corn in their mouths. Even in the rapidly descending darkness he could see all kinds of vegetable gardens around the house. Did his sons own all the trees nearby and the bamboo grove to the east? The whole thing still seemed unreal.

The darkness was becoming dense. Ruhiton could hardly see anything. He could guess that there were people moving about nearby. But he couldn't see any of them. He saw a beam of light approaching. Mangala came into view, a glowing lantern in one hand, an aluminium tumbler in the other. Putting the lantern on the ground, she placed the steaming aluminium glass of tea on the bench. Moving away towards the wooden staircase, she said, 'It's bound to change. Everything has changed. Things are nothing like the way they were when you were here. It's amazing that we're even alive.'

'Yes, I felt the same way,' responded Ruhiton in his nasal voice. 'I was terrified of never seeing any of you again.'

'It was almost like that,' Mangala said. 'Most of them wanted to kill us. We were saved by the grace of Marangburu.'

So Mangala still believed in Marangburu's grace? Had her belief in burning witches come back too? Holding the wicker bowl near his mouth with both his hands, he thrust his tongue in to lick up some corn. The moment his eyes met Mangala's, he closed his mouth hurriedly. She seemed to be staring at him with fear and loathing. Ruhiton forgot to chew.

Trying to smile, he said, 'I cannot eat anything with my hands unless it's soft and mashed. I could have lost my hands entirely if I hadn't been treated.'

'I know, they poisoned you in jail with this illness.'

'No, I realized the truth later,' Ruhiton said, shaking his head. 'Remember our Perwa? He was the one I got this disease from.'

'From Perwa?' Mangala's voice seemed to reverberate. 'All lies!'

'Lies!' said Ruhiton, looking at her with astonishment in his inflamed eyes.

Mangala did not reply. But her face was stiff with suspicion. 'Never mind. What's the use of discussing all this?'

Ruhiton's heart filled with hurt and grief. The entire present seemed like a lie. Yet it was a terrifying reality. Picking the aluminium glass up with both his hands, he sipped the tea. 'Budhua, Karma—where are all of them?'

'They're around somewhere,' Mangala replied. 'They're grown up now, they do as they please. A minister from Delhi is coming to Siliguri, they're busy with the visit.'

Ruhiton felt unable to absorb the implication of what Mangala had said. But the real meaning had penetrated to his core. He looked at Mangala in shock.

'That's why they move around with Kachimuddin these days,' Mangala continued. 'Narsingh Chhetri—he's actually Mohan Chhetri's nephew. He's come from Sikkim to look after the property. Budhua and Karma and all of them are in the same party.'

Ruhiton felt his heart drying up. He understood what Mangala meant. But was there anything he could do about it? He had done what his father had never done. Why should his sons not go their own ways too? Still, he felt the inconsistencies were far more outside jail than within it.

Suddenly he heard snatches of song, accompanied by music. Ruhiton looked questioningly at Mangala. But before she could reply he understood what was going on from the sudden deep voice emanating from a transistor radio. In jail too, they often had music or the radio played for them over loudspeakers.

'Let me take you to the old house,' Mangala said.

'Yes, let's go,' Ruhiton said with a sudden desperation.

Mangala picked up the lantern. 'Can you bring the glass and the bowl?' she asked.

Ruhiton didn't understand why they had to be taken along. Still, he picked the glass up with both his hands and tucked it in under his arm, and, carrying the bowl in both his hands, followed Mangala to the house that had been built in his father's time. The cow was no longer tied to the post. Ruhiton climbed up slowly on the front stoop. He looked at the roof.

'Part of the room on the eastern side is in good shape. I've made all the arrangements there.'

'What arrangements?' Ruhiton asked in surprise.

Mangala looked at him in surprise too, her eyes just like the loving eyes of the cow. But she was no longer as she had been once. 'Why, your living arrangements, of course. I've put a cot in, come and see. We've had the roof on the eastern side rethatched too, with fresh grass. I've put your plates and glass and bowls in there.' She moved with the lantern towards the room on the eastern side.

Ruhiton looked in that direction in the semi-darkness. He didn't seem to understand what Mangala was saying. The aluminium glass was tucked under his arm. He held the woven wicker bowl in his hands.

'Well? Come along.' Mangala's voice floated out.

Ruhiton went forward, treading gingerly with his toeless feet. He entered the house. A pillow and sheets lay on the cot.

'Am I staying here alone? Aren't you staying with me?'

'Me?' Mangala's shadow on the wall seemed to tremble. Going up to the door, she said, 'How can I stay with you? You'll stay separately, just as you did in jail. You can no longer stay with everyone else, can you? I'll bring your food.' Mangala didn't look at Ruhiton directly as she spoke. She looked in turn at his hands and feet, at the wall next to him, at her own shadow. 'You will be looked after properly. By Karam's grace we have all we need now. You'll get milk to drink from the black cow.'

The black cow. 'The deep black eyes of the black cow…' someone used to sing. Ruhiton looked at Mangala. For the first time in his life, he felt that his heart was breaking. But could it really break?

'I'm not ill any more, Mangli,' he said. 'I've recovered. I can live with you, with all of you.' In his nasal voice, the words sounded like a child's petulant demands.

Mangala's face hardened with distrust and annoyance. Her glance was cutting. 'That's obvious from your appearance,' she said. 'Nobody keeps a person at home when they have such illnesses. At least your sons have agreed to let you stay in this old house.'

Looking at Mangala, Ruhiton realized she was saying all this with deep conviction. Ruhiton had believed that towns could be encircled with villages. Those who shared this belief had destroyed everything around them in their conviction. But what was this torrent again in his heart? He hobbled a couple of steps forward, his eyes on Mangala. Her eyes were apprehensive, wary. She made to leave.

'Have you married again?' Ruhiton asked.

Mangala's eyes twinkled. Then she laughed, covering her mouth with her hand, her body shaking. 'Does it look as though I've married again?' she asked, uncovering her mouth.

Ruhiton could not answer when he saw her laughing. By the light of the lantern, he did not look entirely human. His eyelids, shorn of lashes, were red and unblinking.

'No, I've had no such wish ever,' Mangala continued.

Ruhiton was torn between happiness and pain. With hope as well as despair, he said, 'Do you remember those days, Mangli? That time of our Liberated Zone?'

Mangala frowned, her face tight. 'What's the use of remembering all that? I don't remember them any more.'

Someone could be heard talking outside before Mangala had finished. She looked over her shoulder. Then retreated a few steps. She looked at Ruhiton again. 'I'd better go,' she said. 'Budhua's wife Mangri is cooking all by herself. I'll bring your food when it's time.' Turning around, Mangala disappeared in the darkness.

Ruhiton remained rooted to the spot. Who had called Mangala away? It was a male voice. Was it one of his sons? Or someone else? There was no one to answer.

The lantern cast a steady glow, his shadow was still. Crickets shrilled somewhere in the thatched roof overhead. Ruhiton turned around. The western side of the house had collapsed on its face. His childhood days floated up before his eyes. His adolescent days. His mother used to live there at the back. There used to be oxen behind the fence. There was a different smell in this room then.

He looked at the open door again. Mangala had left. That old song of his mother's rang in his ears. 'Clouds gather in the north, it's raining in the west.' What a life! Clouds gather here, it rains somewhere else. The fine clothes of life only get wet.

Chapter Nineteen

Late night in the Terai. Who knew how late it was? Ruhiton lay on his bedstead in the impenetrable darkness in his room. Mangala had served him his dinner in his separate plate and bowl. 'Have your dinner,' she had said. 'Lock the door.' She had pulled the door shut when leaving.

Yes, a child of the Kurmis and Mahatos never quarrelled with his meal. But can every meal be eaten, O son of a Mahato? He didn't have that kind of appetite. He hadn't been able to eat. He had only gazed at Mangala as long as she had been there. He couldn't smell her familiar scent. He no longer had nostrils, but still, he had inhaled deeply.

Ruhiton had soon become aware that a dog had entered, pushing the door open, and that the animal was eating his dinner with greedy, surprised trepidation. He had been thinking of a particular story that Mangala had told him several times. The story, told in her voice, rang in his ears.

'And then…yes, and then the husband told his wife, sprinkle this magic water on me, I'll turn into a gigantic crocodile. And then when you sprinkle the water on me again, I'll go back to being a human being. Is that even possible, wondered the wife. Can magic water do such things? Let me check. Tilting the pot, she sprinkled the water on her husband. At once he turned into a giant crocodile. He was a terrifying sight. The wife tried to run away from the crocodile. And the pot overturned when she tripped over it, all the water spilled out…

'And then? Ah ha! Then the crocodile could no longer be turned back into a human being. Hs wife looked at him anxiously from a distance, she didn't dare go near him. Thus the days went by. But the man was a crocodile now. How long could he starve? Tears rolled out of his eyes from hunger and sadness. His wife didn't understand. Then the crocodile left his home, crawled across the courtyard and submerged himself in a lake nearby. He ate plenty of fish, finally satiating his hunger.

'His wife came and stood at the edge of the water. The crocodile surfaced. Approaching the shore, he looked at his wife. How shall I get you back, dear, his wife asked. The crocodile could not talk. There was nothing to say anyway. The magic water was not within reach any more…

'Days went by, one after the other. The wife came to the lake and sat at the edge of the water for a glimpse of her husband. The crocodile surfaced from time to time. He looked at his wife, then dived back into the depths. The rest of their life passed this way. The crocodile's wife kept sitting at the edge of the water, the crocodile surfaced at times to gaze at her…'

That was all there was to the story. Mangala's voice would drift into sleep. Ruhiton couldn't stop thinking of this tale.

Then, in the undisturbed darkness of the night, Ruhiton sat up in bed. Treading carefully on his toeless feet, he went outside the house. The sleeping Terai night was far advanced. Stars twinkled on the black canvas of the sky. He came out in the open and looked up to the west. He couldn't see Venus. Had it disappeared behind the trees? A few scattered spots of light were visible on the northern hills, just like the stars. He began walking to the east.

Adhikari Baba's lake came into view. Even eight years ago, on the eastern side of the lake, beyond its high periphery, the area leading to the Mechi had been a jungle. Ruhiton had buried something as his last possession under the earth in that jungle. Was it still there? Lots of people lived around the lake now. Adhikari Baba's temple was always crowded. Rituals and fairs were organized in January. People here vowed to sacrifice animals and birds to the gods if their prayers were met. But they were not actually slaughtered, only let loose by the lake, which was huge. The thick vines on the surface of the black water made one afraid to wade in. Nobody fished here.

Ruhiton kept walking. He had a long way to walk. To Moynaguri village. The railway line passed nearby. A bridge ran over it. Ruhiton forced himself to move as quickly as possible. He knew the way. It ran through the fields—a secret trail.

The road refused to end. Suddenly he heard a gurgling sound. The sound of the currents on the Mechi. Had a pale glow appeared in the eastern sky? That would mean trouble. But there it was, the edge of the lake! There was still a thick growth of trees there. Ruhiton was perspiring profusely. Even the wind that blew the night away couldn't dry his sweat. He remembered where the paved edge of the lake, with the steps leading down to the water, lay. He went in the opposite direction. He couldn't walk up the steep slope of the lake. He climbed on his hands and knees instead. Where was that Arjuna tree? No one had cut it in all this time, had they? The land had not been swept away, had it?

Crawling up the slope, Ruhiton reached the top and straightened slowly. The eastern sky seemed to be looking a little pale. He spotted the Arjuna tree. It was there! Then perhaps everything was intact. He hobbled up to the tree. He glanced at the slope leading back to the edge of the water.

But he had no spade or crowbar with him. Looking around, he spotted the branch of a tree. Clutching it in both his paws, he walked down the slope. His heart was beating furiously. Wonderful! It was there—the rock marking the spot was still in place! The earth had subsided slightly under torrents of rain. But the rock was still wedged in. Diba babu had known of this spot.

Moving the rock aside with his feet, Ruhiton sat down in the depression it had left. He almost missed his footing. Lying down flat to prevent himself from rolling down the slope, he began to dig at the ground with the branch in his paws. So hard? It was like stone. But he mustn't stop. As he kept digging, he hit soft earth. A hole appeared in the soil. The earth rolled down the sides. At that moment he spotted a part of the object. Lying on his stomach, Ruhiton inserted both his arms, holding the butt of the gun between his paws. It couldn't be pulled out easily. After much effort, a double-barrelled gun emerged. The earth fell away. A small box was visible.

Holding the gun between his knees, Ruhiton lifted the box. It was made of thick board, which crumbled under his touch. Bullets lay inside it. Picking them up in his paws, he sniffed the bullets. The sodden smell of earth. Soggy. He lifted the gun. Faint light streamed through the trees. He saw holes eaten into the wooden butt by termites. Both the barrels were jammed with earth.

Ruhiton placed a third of what was left of his right index finger on the trigger. Pressing the butt against his chest, he squeezed the trigger with his withered finger. A rusty sound emerged. But the trigger moved. This withered finger was still able to squeeze a trigger! Would this gun work again if it were dried in the sun? Would the bullets fire? If the earth could be cleared from the barrels, would they shoot bullets?

Ruhiton was panting and perspiring profusely. His tongue was hanging out. No, it wasn't possible to remain sitting here any longer. His lungs did not seem capable of holding air. He lay down slowly. He tilted his head, resting them on the barrels. His reddened eyelids, shorn of lashes, dropped. He had just one consolation now: he had returned to his real place from the humiliation and the accursed shelter he had been provided. He could sense that waves of a deep slumber were washing over him now.

The black water of the enormous lake shimmered in the breeze. Sudden streaks of silver appeared among the dense vines on its surface. Amidst the tendrils on the deep, dark water, the silver streaks curved away sharply.